THE ADVENTURES OF ARTHUR PENNINGTON

✕

OPERATION GOLDEN GOAL

THE ADVENTURES OF ARTHUR PENNINGTON

✕

OPERATION GOLDEN GOAL

PHILIP HARTLEY

ISBN-13: 979-8672917474

CONTENTS:

I   Westminster Warriors..........................7

II   The Key...16

III   School...26

IV   Back on Track...............................40

V   Fire...52

VI   Butch..72

VII   Momentum....................................86

VIII Trains..94

IX   The Geography Field Trip.................107

X   Football...121

XI   The Capital City Stadium....................137

XII   Homecoming....................................156

CHAPTER 1

Westminster Warriors

My name's Arthur, but most people call me Artie (or Arty - I'm not sure how to 'officially' spell it). Everyone began calling me Artie when I was younger, which really confused me. Originally, I assumed that people called me this because they thought that I was good at painting art pictures. This is where the confusion came in, as I was probably the worst artist in my class. One time when I was five I painted a picture of a car. I was really proud of this painting and so I decided to stand up on my stool, and show it off to everyone in the class. Unfortunately though, nearly the whole class (including the teacher) mistook it for an elephant (the only person who didn't think it was an elephant was Vernon, who thought that I had painted a spaceship). I was distraught after this because up until this moment, I really did think that I had the potential to

7

become a professional artist, similar to Leonardo da Vinci. To make matters worse, I lost my balance while I was standing on the stool and fell, breaking my arm in the process. Ouch.

Anyway, once people began to call me Artie, I would write my name on my school work with the letters 'RT', as it sounded just like Artie (and I also thought that it looked really cool). However, people then thought that this stood for my initials and became confused as to what my actual name was. So now I just write Arthur on all of my school work, yet people still call me Artie.

Speaking of school, I do find school really tough sometimes. For five days a week and for thirty-nine weeks of the year, I have to spend loads of money on train tickets just to get there. For most days, I don't even want to go, it's just that apparently the law says that I have to and that if I don't, my parents would probably go to prison. Come to think of it that wouldn't be so bad; I would be able to play computer games whenever I wanted to, in addition to eating food in the lounge without anyone stopping me. You see, my dad says that I'm not allowed to eat there, as he thinks that I "make a mess". This is really ironic though, as one time, when we were watching a football match together (I think Westminster Warriors were playing against AFC Hartford), he spilled his coffee all over the sofa. This was a tough situation, especially considering that we had only had the sofa for one-week. To make matters worse, I missed a spectacular goal (deemed as "the goal of the century" by most football fans) from Roger Jenkins while we were desperately trying to remove the stain. Although it has slightly faded, the coffee stain still remains. Whenever I see the stain, it reminds me of the time I missed "the goal of the century" from Roger Jenkins live on TV.

Jenkins was definitely my favourite footballer growing up. I even got his shirt once from when I went to a Westminster Warriors game - it was at a match in August when I was 8 years old. I remember the day really well because it was my first visit to London. I had always wanted to go to London because of the famous landmarks. One of my favourite landmarks in particular is Tower Bridge. I just think that it looks really cool and iconic. Although it looks awesome, I think they could have been a bit more creative in naming it. I mean, calling it 'Tower Bridge' is like calling Big Ben 'The Clock Tower'.

Anyway, the reason we visited London was because we found some cheap tickets for a midweek cup game vs. Nottingham Friday. I was so excited for the game. After concluding our tour of London with a visit to Westminster Abbey, my dad and I headed over to the James Benjamin Stadium, the venue for the match. Shortly after we had arrived, I discovered that Roger Jenkins was going to be starting on the substitute's bench for the game, as he was being 'rested' for a league match vs. Worcestershire United. Regardless, the match was very exciting. Before the match, I thought that Nottingham Friday would be easy opponents for Westminster, especially considering that they were bottom of League 3. In fact, Westminster were probably fortunate to finish the first half with the scores level at 0-0.

The second half was a lot closer, with both teams missing many chances to score. In the 80th minute of the game the match was still 0-0, with the game heading towards extra-time The Nottingham players began to significantly tire, and it was clear that they had chosen to 'park the bus'. This is where a team has all of their players behind the ball (apart from their striker) in the hope of drawing a match or holding onto a win. It's usually what weaker teams do when they play against one of the stronger teams. I think that Nottingham were hoping to take the game to a penalty shootout, as it was probably their best chance of progressing to the next round.

As the game approached the 90 minute mark, Charlie Trundle took a shot from 40 yards out. The ball looked like it was going to soar into the top corner, yet somehow the Friday goalkeeper produced a flying fingertip save to keep the ball out. Somehow the score was still 0-0. As Trundle was walking over to take the resulting corner, he soon had to turn around, as the fourth official held up his number to signal a substitution. A world class player left the field in Trundle, but a legend came on to take his place: Jenkins had arrived!

Jenkins rushed onto the field to a rousing reception. He ran straight into the 18-yard box, ready for the corner ball that was about to be taken. Micky Ryan walked over to take the corner ball. He produced a delightful ball into the box towards the near post. Alfie Morgan managed to flick the ball towards the goal. The ball raced towards the back post, into the path of Jenkins, who diverted the ball towards the goal with a diving header. The ball nestled into the bottom corner of the goal. The crowd roared as the goal went in. That was the goal we had all been waiting for!

Once things had calmed down after the match, I was desperate to buy a Jenkins shirt from the club store. We were going to go to the store after the game (if it was open) to buy one. However, before we were about to leave, we noticed the Westminster team come over to the stand that we were in, as they were applauding the fans for their support. To my amazement, Jenkins then signalled that he was going to give his shirt away. As he was about to throw the shirt into the crowd, I knew that this was my chance. I did not want to miss this opportunity of getting a shirt off Roger Jenkins. When Jenkins threw the shirt, it felt as if time stood still. My mind was solely focused on the shirt, and from predicting the trajectory of the shirt's flight, it looked as if it would end up in the second row, two rows in front of where my dad and I were sitting. For a nanosecond, disappointment clouded my mind, as it seemed that I would not be able to capitalise on this opportunity. Yet, I was not going to give up without a fight. Importantly, the feeling of disappointment soon triggered a sense of desperation. Adrenaline rushed through my body, inciting me to do something that I did not thing that I was capable of. Without hesitation, I climbed onto the man in front of me, stood on his shoulders, and took a giant leap for the shirt. For a few seconds I was in mid-air with my prized possession. I felt like a superhero.

Crunch. The feeling of bliss was short-lived, as I found myself lying on the floor by the advertising hoardings next to an injured Micky Ryan. He was probably Westminster's second-best player after Jenkins, and he was giving someone in the front row an autograph before I had inadvertently landed on him, injuring him in the process. It was a shame because he had twisted his knee in the fall, which ruled him out for the rest of that season. This was a disaster for Westminster, as he was the club's record signing at the time, and to make matters worse, he had only made two appearances for the club.

I couldn't really remember what happened in the aftermath of Ryan getting injured – I think I fell unconscious. It wasn't until someone showed me a viral video clip of what had happened, when I was at school the following morning, that I was able to comprehend the gravity of the overall situation. My memory was slightly clouded about what had happened until I saw the video clip, as when I had woken up the following morning, I thought that me falling on Ryan was a dream (or a nightmare). As soon as I saw the clip, memories of what had happened at the match flooded into my head.

There were news reports on me injuring Ryan all over the internet, in addition to videos that had gone viral. The video that I saw reached 1.8 million views in less than 24 hours! After replaying the video numerous times, I was relieved to see that the cameras didn't get a view of my face that was clear enough in order for me to be identified. It probably helped that I was wearing a snood, in addition to having my hood up.

I also owe a lot of gratitude to my dad, as while everyone was focusing on Micky Ryan, he quickly picked me up and rushed towards the exit. Things didn't exactly go smoothly from this point onwards, as he had aroused a lot of suspicion amongst the matchday stewards. I guess they had presumed that I was being kidnapped or something. Once my dad noticed that the stewards were approaching him, he panicked, before dashing towards the exit as quickly as he could. This triggered a domino effect, as they began to run after him in response, to try and keep up with him. This caught the attention of the crowd, with some of the supporters joining in with the stewards in chasing him down.

Fortunately, my dad (still holding me) had managed to get a good head start on his adversaries, and once he had managed to escape from the stadium, darted towards the nearest tube station as fast as he could (fortunately, it was only 90 seconds away). Shortly after he left the stadium, a trail of people who were chasing him emerged from the stadium behind him. It was important that he got onto the tube before anyone could catch him. 'A crowd draws a crowd', and as the trail of people pierced through the streets, more people joined in the chase.

Immediately on arriving at the tube station, my dad quickly climbed over the barriers, before sliding down the side of the escalator like a superspy. He reached the tube platform just in time, and as he boarded the tube, one of the security officers who worked at the tube station, dived towards him, managing to grab hold of his foot as the door was closing. It looked as if it was 'game over'. Nevertheless, my dad managed to wriggle his foot free, albeit losing a shoe as a result.

Amusingly, I was at the heart of the action while this was all happening, yet I didn't know about it until the following day when I came home from school. I don't even know how much of the story my dad was exaggerating, but from the videos I've seen, his description of the events seem pretty accurate! Maybe it wouldn't be good if my parents went to jail after all, as they do a lot for me, even if I don't always realise it.

CHAPTER 2

The Key

So as I was saying, I find school really tough sometimes, and after a tough day at school last Wednesday, my parents announced to my sister and I that they would be away at a conference for Thursday evening and Friday morning. It seemed that they didn't want to tell us what it was about – all they would say was that it was "important". Just for the record, I'm not entirely sure what my parents do for a living, I mean, I know that they work in an office, but that's about it. My mum usually comes back home at about 4 p.m., my dad doesn't come back until about 6 p.m. and it's not often that they both go away for the night.

As they were going to be away for a whole night, I recognised that the occasion presented a prime opportunity for me to do what I could do if my parents went to prison: play computer games. You see, my parents strongly discourage me from playing computer games, as apparently, they're bad for 'brain development' or something like that. (About 5 years ago my dad read a newspaper article titled "why you should never allow your child to play computer games".) I wanted to make the most of the occasion. I wanted it to be special, so I decided that I would invite some of my friends over to play football in real life, and on my computer game console.

For my console, we currently have the MegaWay 5 at home. I've had it for about 6 years, as my Grandma gave it to me for Christmas when I was 7. She said that I could have whatever I wanted for that Christmas, as she forgot to get me a birthday present in the same year. Without any second thoughts, I asked for the MegaWay 5, as this was what all of my friends were playing at the time. When I got the MegaWay 5, I was excited to spend the rest of the Christmas holidays playing computer games. However, after the holidays my dad soon warned me that I would only be allowed to use the MegaWay 5 on Fridays. For the rest of week, the MegaWay 5 was to be locked away in a cupboard in my house somewhere. It was therefore important that I could find the key for the cupboard!

Originally, I thought that it would be very difficult to find the key, yet it proved to be a straightforward task, as the key was in a drawer, next to the cupboard. Instead of using the key to open the cupboard and get the console ready for the evening, I did something else. You see, if I took the console my plan would have been scuppered, as I know that my parents always check the cupboard to see if I have taken the console before they go out together, while they usually take the key with them as well.

My plan was to get a cutting of the key. The key cutting shop, *Kurt's Keys*, usually closes at 6 p.m., so in order to get there before it closed, I had to miss some of my mum's special cake for pudding. It wasn't too bad, as I was able to have some once I came back. My mum also made another cake for Katie (my older sister) and I, as supposedly, we were going to be on our own at home together on Thursday. This was awesome, as my mum is the best at making cake.

I think the best cake that my mum has ever made was probably from about 5 years ago. The cake was topped with caramel spread and chocolate buttons. It also had two layers which had been joined together with some Hibblesbury jam, and a good amount of whipped cream. The texture was perfect, the density was flawless, and I honestly think that this cake was so good that the majority of adjectives in the

English language fail to do it justice. When it comes to baking cakes, my mum is probably one of the best in the country, and on this day, she got everything concerning the cake spot on. The reason for having the cake was because we were celebrating the fact that I had finally managed to get my swimming certificate after 5 years. This was a big deal for me as there were some tough moments that I had to endure. For instance, there was this one time where I nearly drowned. If it wasn't for one of the lifeguards, I would probably have died. That was about 9 years ago, and the same lifeguard still works at the same leisure centre today. I think that maybe I should thank him sometime, but then again, he might find it weird if I did as he probably wouldn't remember me, as he's probably saved many other kids since he saved me.

Anyway, as I was saying *Kurt's Keys* usually closes at 6 p.m., and once I had finished eating my dinner, I only had 7 minutes to get to the store in time. I didn't want my parents to know about me going out, as I didn't want them to know about my plan. As we eat our meals in the Dining Room, which is very close to the front door, I didn't think that I was able to go out of this door without being heard. Unfortunately, the back door was also locked, and I wasn't sure where the key was, and I also didn't have enough time to go traipsing around the house looking for it. While deciding the course of action that I should take, 35 precious seconds had passed by, meaning that I was then left with 6 minutes and 25 seconds to get to the store before it closed. Swiftly, I rushed into the nearby lounge, closed the door behind, and scrambled out of the window before scurrying over to the pavement to make a bold dash for the shop, hoping that nobody in the house would notice me. I doubted that they would, as they probably had their attention fixated on the glorious cake that my mum had made.

According to an app on my phone, it takes approximately 10 minutes to walk to *Kurt's Keys* from my home - I wasn't sure whether I would arrive in time. Partway along the route, I had to cross Kourston Road. During the day, this road is relatively quiet; however between 5 p.m. and 6:30 p.m., it gets very busy, making it very difficult to cross without getting hit by one of the cars. Not long after I reached Kourston Road, I soon managed to comprehend the magnitude of the challenging situation that awaited me. With a car zooming past every time I attempted to cross the road, the probability of me doing something rash seemingly increased. After being stranded at the crossing for 42 seconds, I had had enough and theorised that I would be able to avoid the cars if I ran fast enough. I soon noticed a small break up in the traffic and decided to run as fast as I could to the other side of the road. I darted into the middle of the road. I then pulled out a little dance move, as I thought that I was going to make it to the other side of the road unscathed. Whilst I was dancing and running in the middle of the road, a speedy electric sports car was zooming along the road and clipped my ankle, flipping me into mid-air.

Fortunately, because I was in the middle of a special dance, I had a little 'spring in my step' meaning that milliseconds before the car drove into me, I was in a good position to jump – and that's exactly what I did. I reckon my legs would have had to have been amputated or something if I didn't jump. Also, it helped that the car was low in height, as it meant that it only clipped my heel. If it was a chunky SUV, the situation would probably have been a lot worse. When I was flying through the air after getting clipped, I managed to swivel my legs and perfectly execute a somersault onto the pavement, coming away from the incident relatively unscathed. I was very fortunate to come away from this incident uninjured - this was probably one of the stupidest things that I have done. From this moment onwards, I always make sure that the coast is clear before I cross a road, as it's not worth risking a serious injury in order to avoid being late for something.

This situation also effectively demonstrated the importance of school, as in PE, we're currently learning the ins and outs of trampolining, with the somersault being a significant part of our recent lessons. You see, during some lessons at school I sometimes ask myself: "why am I learning this, what's the point"? This was the case soon after I had discovered that we were going to be trampolining in PE instead of football. At the time I was annoyed and frustrated, as not only did I think that trampolining was uncool, but I also thought that it was completely pointless. However, I soon began to enjoy it, and if we hadn't have done it, I probably wouldn't have been able to somersault onto the pavement when I got hit by the car. Seconds after landing, I glanced at my watch: the time was 17:59:12 and I was about 60 yards away from the shop.

As I approached *Kurt's Keys*, I could see that the shopkeeper (presumably his name was Kurt) was about to put the sign up in the door reading 'closed'. Because I was approaching the store at a high velocity, I didn't have enough time to slow down - I thought that I was about to smash into the door (or through it). Thankfully, Kurt abruptly opened the door in time. Phew.

Once I had caught my breath and thanked Kurt for letting me in, I asked him about getting the key cut. Originally, he told me that it would cost £20. I laughed. I thought that £20 to get a key cut was ridiculous, but apparently he offered "the best prices in Wiltshire". Reluctantly, I coughed up the £20.

I was a lot more cautious on the way back home. Although I had to wait at the crossing on Kourston Road for 3 minutes, it was better than going through the range of emotions that I had previously experienced. After safely crossing the road and strolling along the pavement, I was finally home...but there was a slight problem: the window that I had climbed out of was closed, and all of the doors were locked. I didn't knock on the door, as I didn't want anyone to know that I had been out. Instead, I went into the back garden, and I was relieved to see that I had left my bedroom window open. Although my window was open, I needed to figure out how I was going to climb up.

As the garden shed was comfortably positioned next to the house (and close to my window), I saw it as a way for me to get up to the window. I also needed to figure how I was going to climb onto the shed. For this, I put some wheelie bins between the house and the shed. In addition to this, I also placed some bed sheets (that were hanging on the washing line) on top of the bins to try and make things a bit safer (And yes, I did wash the sheets afterwards). Once I was on the shed, the gap between the shed and my window looked as if it had grown since I had climbed up. I needed to jump. It wasn't a very big jump, and I also knew that I would be okay if I fell (due to the positioning of the bins and the bed sheets), but still, the fact that I needed to jump was a bit daunting. I did it. After jumping, I managed to successfully hold onto the window sill. I then lurched myself through the window, before crashing onto the floor.

Shortly after revelling in the success of the mission, I heard a knock on my door. All of a sudden, a river of dismay rushed into my mind, extinguishing the kindle of delight that had illuminated my being, prior to the dreaded knock. I thought that it was my parents. I thought that they had discovered what had happened. It felt like it was game over. There was a second knock. This time it was louder, and slightly more aggressive than the first. Reluctantly, I picked myself up and went over to the door to open it. To my relief it was Katie.

I thought that she was going to ask me about my trip, but instead she just asked about my plans for Thursday evening. At first, I was hesitant to tell her, but after she told me that one of her friends had invited her over on Thursday evening for some sort of 'revision evening', meaning that I would have the house to myself, I realised that it didn't matter if I let her know.

Soon after I had finished talking to Katie, my parents came up to my room to tell me that because I was going to be home alone, they would let me use the MegaWay 5 on Thursday evening. They even encouraged me to invite friends over! I guess that I should have just asked them in the beginning instead of unnecessarily spending £20 on a key. They also gave me a spare key for the house. It was nice to be treated like an adult for once.

CHAPTER 3

School

Thursday soon arrived, and I was excited for the day ahead. From the moment I woke up, I was thrilled about the prospect of having the whole house to myself. Due to the overall enthusiasm that I had to start the day, I woke up 2 hours earlier than usual. This meant that I also arrived at school earlier than I usually would, as I normally arrive at school just before it starts.

After waiting in the school dining room on my own for 30 minutes, some other kids from my year group arrived. I was fed up with being on my own, so even though I didn't particularly like some of the people who had just arrived at school, I decided to go over and hang out with them anyway. I went over and some of the kids looked surprised - and the situation soon felt a bit awkward. Someone then pushed me in the back, causing me to spill some orange juice on Keith's brand-new trainers. Keith was one of the popular tough guys in our year group, and if there was one person in particular who I didn't want to spill orange juice over, it was Keith. In retaliation, Keith gave me a monster wedgie in front of everyone. Not only was I highly embarrassed, but I also had to find a spare pair of boxers, as the sheer force of the wedgie caused my pants to rip. Don't get me wrong, I did want to fight back against Keith, but at the same time I didn't want to end up with a broken nose.

At my school, the only place where you can find spare clothing is the school lost property basket (which is actually just a wheelie bin located in the PE changing rooms). So, after being humiliated by Keith, I went over to the PE changing rooms to looks for a spare pair of underwear. I found some. They were the perfect size for me, but they also smelled. I think that they had been in the lost property basket for a while, as they were right at the very bottom of the bin. Amongst the lost clothes was a 'leavers jumper' from 2008. I think that this may have meant that the pants had been in lost property for at least 10 years. You may be thinking that it was disgusting for me to even think about wearing the pants, but I did end up putting them on, and they were actually quite comfy.

To counteract the smell, I scrubbed the pants under the shower before holding them under the hand dryer. I also sprayed them with some of my deodorant.

Once I had put the pants on, I went back to the wheelie bin to have another look at the leaver's jumper from 2008. I thought it would be cool to see if I recognised any of the names on the back. The fact that this was about 10 years old fascinated me, as I have always had a deep interest in objects from the past. I think it's because I like to see how things change over time. In fact, this kind of relates to what I want to do when I'm older, as I want to be an explorer who travels the world, exploring new and intriguing places. I'm an adventurer at heart. I was about to take another look at the jumper, but before I was able to the school bell started to ring. This was a shame, as I desperately wanted to examine the jumper, yet I also recognised that I needed to be patient – I didn't want to be late for morning tutor.

Later, when the bell rang for morning break, I went straight to the lost property bin. I opened up the lid of the bin and reached in to pick out the jumper. As I was rummaging through the clothes in lost property, I heard footsteps from outside the changing rooms. I didn't know who was coming into the changing rooms, so I was happy when I realised that it was just Vernon and Ricky.

Vernon and Ricky were my best mates. It was convenient that they had both come to hang out with me, as it gave me an opportunity to talk to them about my plan for the evening. They were excited about the plan, but there attention was primarily focused on why I was trawling through lost property. I was going to explain what I was doing, but I didn't need to, as I soon found the jumper near the bottom of the pile. I then lay the jumper out on one of the changing room benches for us to observe. The name 'Jenko' was sprawled across the back, along with a huge '08', made up of the names of everyone from the year 11 class of 2008.

I glanced across the names to see if any of them stood out. I didn't think that any would, but when I got to the surnames beginning with the latter 'J', one of the names unexpectedly jumped out at me. At first, I wasn't even sure if I had imagined that the name was on the jumper, or if it was actually there. I quickly asked Vernon and Ricky to have a look, and to my content agreed with me that the name was...Roger Jenkins! We then came to the realisation that the jumper probably belonged to Jenkins himself, as people probably called him Jenko as a nickname (hence the jumper having 'Jenko' written across the back of it). Also, he would have been 16 years old in 2008, which is the age that people finish school (unless they stay on to go to the sixth form). I found it quite cool how I was actually holding the jumper that belonged to one of the best footballers in the world.

It's awesome that Roger Jenkins actually went to the same school as me. I think that this is probably why the sports hall is named after him, and why there are loads of pictures of him dotted around the school. I thought that this was just because he was a great footballer – I didn't think that he actually went to the same school as me. I wanted to take the jumper home and sell it on the internet, as I reckon that I could have auctioned it off for a high price. However, Ricky said that this would technically be stealing as the jumper didn't actually belong to me. Vernon then suggested that I tag Roger Jenkins into a social media post about me finding the jumper. This was good for two reasons: firstly we could definitively know whether the jumper was actually Jenkins', and also we were going to cheekily ask him if we could keep it. Therefore, it wouldn't be stealing if he gave it to us.

So, I sent out a public message on social media and tagged Roger Jenkins' account. The message read: "Hey Roger, just found your old leaver's jumper in our school's lost property bin. Am I alright to have it"? I also attached a picture of the jumper so that people didn't think that I was lying. To my amazement, Jenkins ended up replying to my post within 10 minutes. Not only did he let me keep the jumper, but he also offered to sign it at the English Cup Final, as Westminster Warriors were playing Hibblesbury Rovers on Saturday at the Capital City Stadium. After following me on social media, Jenkins then offered me some VIP seats for myself and a guest, which included special access. I guess this was so that I was able to get the jumper signed by him.

Awkwardly, I wasn't sure who I should invite to the game out of Vernon and Ricky, as they both wanted the spare ticket. I did think about buying another ticket, but in order for one of them to sit with me, it would have to be a VIP ticket which cost about £150-£200. I couldn't decide, so in the end I cheekily sent Jenkins a DM explaining the situation. Unsurprisingly, Jenkins was cool about the whole situation, and just gave me another VIP all-access ticket. It was really awesome that he did this, and I did feel that it was rude of me to ask him for another ticket when he had just given me two. But then again, £200 is probably peanuts to him (considering that he earns about £200,000 a week from his football contract alone).

We then left the PE changing rooms and headed towards the school field to play some football.

While eating a delicious caramel-topped flapjack on my way to the field, Mr Greasley came out of nowhere to tell me that I had a detention for using my phone at school. He said that he knew that I was on my phone as he noticed that my social media post had been trending online. This was annoying, but at the same time I didn't really care.

When we got to the school field there was only about seven minutes left of our morning break, yet there was still enough time for me to join in on a game of Wembley singles. In case you don't know, Wembley singles is an elimination-style game that we frequently play at our school. Each player has to score a goal to progress to the next round. Once someone scores a goal, they then have to leave the field. The last player on the field to not have scored a goal is then eliminated from the consequent rounds. This happens until there are only two players left who then face off against each other.

When I joined the game, I decided to employ the tactic of goal-hanging. I did this so that I didn't get sweaty for when I'm in class, as sitting in sweaty school uniform can be incredibly uncomfortable. I didn't want to get sweaty on this day in particular, as I'm trying to impress a girl called Elise who I sit next to in science class on Thursday. I'm pretty sure that she wouldn't appreciate sitting next to a guy who stinks of BO.

Anyway, everyone was beginning to get annoyed with me goal-hanging, as apparently I was 'stealing' other people's goals. The last straw was when Connor, who's basically the best footballer in our year group, skilfully dribbled past 5 players, did a few flashy stepovers, before running around the keeper and tapping the ball towards what he thought was an empty net. He then began to wheel away in celebration as if he had just scored a goal for England.

His mood suddenly changed when he turned around and saw me tap the ball into the goal from less than a yard out (as I was standing on the goal line all along). Like a hungry leopard eyeing up his prey, Connor looked at me with a frightening expression that sent shivers down by spine. I was scared. All of a sudden, he then started to chase me, and as I didn't want to spend a night in the hospital, I also ran.

I actually surprised myself at how fast I was able to run. Maybe I could improve on my time of 15.2 seconds in the 100m sprint if I had someone chasing me while I was doing it!

While running as fast as I could through the school field like a wounded hyena being chased by an angry buffalo, I turned around and noticed that other people who were playing football had joined in on the chase. Some of them were my mates who were trying to stop Connor, while the rest were probably just as frustrated with my goal hanging tactics as Connor was. It looked like a potential civil war was on the verge of breaking out between the year 9 footballers.

At this point I decided to make a run for the woods that bordered the school field. My plan was to climb the Duncan tree. This was a tree that was planted by Michael Duncan on the day of the school's opening 254 years ago, and due to the tree's structure (and the formation of the branches), it is relatively easy to climb. About 20 yards away from the forest, I glanced behind to see how close Connor was, and to my shock he was less than 5 metres away. I thought that he was going to catch me, I thought that it was game over, but from somewhere within I managed to find an extra burst of energy. I think that it was from the scrumptious caramel-topped flapjack that I had consumed on my way to the field!

I then sprinted at a speed that I didn't think I was capable of. This has made me ponder whether I could become a flapjack-powered superhero, as when I eat a flapjack, I feel like I have been enhanced with some special powers. I'm not sure what my name would be, but I'm thinking of something like Flappy Jack, or maybe one that's darker like 'The Night-Shadow'.

I entered the woods and headed straight for the Duncan tree. As soon as I had gone past the first set of trees, a feeling of eeriness seemingly trickled into the surrounding atmosphere (and the fact that Connor was hot on my heels didn't make the situation any easier for me to bear). I soon approached the Duncan tree, and as the branches were quite low down it wasn't too hard for me to climb. After frantically climbing, I soon found myself safely poised on a branch 20 ft. above the ground.

Approximately 5 seconds later, Connor and everyone else arrived at the scene. Connor then demanded that I climb down from the tree and "face up to him like a man". After refusing to climb down for a beating, he then started to call me a "chicken". I still refused to come down, yet I soon came to the realisation that I would have to come down eventually, especially as there was only 2 minutes of break left at this point. While I was thinking of what to do next, someone surprised Connor with a spear move, causing him to fall to the ground. Connor then fought back, resulting in a brawl amongst the year 9 footballers (along with others who had followed us into the woods).

As everyone's attention had seemingly diverted away from me, I saw a gleaming opportunity for me to escape the sticky situation that I had found myself in. I then proceeded to climb down the tree with speed and patience. Once I had climbed down, I began to walk away before transitioning into a sprint, as I thought that I had successfully eluded Connor and co. However, when I started to run away, Bernie, one of Connor's best friends, quickly alerted everybody of my attempt at escaping. Suddenly, everyone began to chase after me, with Connor soon emerging at the front of the group.

At this point I felt exhausted and I recognised that it was highly unlikely that I would be able to outrun Connor again. Nevertheless, I still decided to carry on running – I wasn't going to give in easily. I was running as fast as I could, yet Connor soon caught up with me and rugby-tackled me to the ground. Ouch. I thought that he was going to beat me up while I was on the floor, but he didn't. He stood back and allowed me to stand up.

Everyone else then circled around us, forming a fighting ring in the process. I hadn't ever been in a fight before, nor had I done any fight-related training

– I didn't know what to do. Connor then came towards me and threw a jab. I managed to sway to my left. He threw another punch, which I then blocked with my wrist before counterpunching him in the face. This unnerved him a bit, and I think that everyone was shocked that I had managed to connect a punch so sweetly. This moment of glory was short lived though, as Connor came back at me with more aggression, striking me with a powerful punch to my face. Pow. I instantaneously fell to the floor. I had never been hit with such ferocity before.

Fortunately, I didn't get knocked out, and I decided to stay on the floor as I didn't want to get up for another potential beating. Suddenly, Connor got a few sachets of ketchup out of his bag and then squirted the contents of them onto his face. I thought that this was strange behaviour and began to wonder whether I was imagining it.

It didn't take long for me to come to terms with the details of the new situation that had arisen, as it turned out that Connor was faking an injury in an attempt at deceiving the vice-principle, Mr. Greasley, who had arrived at the scene. He was furious. Connor then told Mr Greasley a twisted story of what had unfolded. Somehow, Mr Greasley actually believed everything the Connor said. As a result, Connor avoided punishment, while I was given a detention, as apparently I was the one who caused all of the trouble! Even though everyone else was 15 minutes late for class, all they got was 'a warning'. I didn't want to go down without telling Mr Greasley what actually happened, so I told him that Connor had just squirted ketchup on his face to make it look like I had caused him to bleed. Mr Greasley brushed my claims aside refusing to believe me, and to make things worse, he threatened me with another detention for being "disrespectful" towards him.

I think that Connor got special treatment from Mr Greasley due to his position as the captain of the school rugby team. The rugby team had an important semi-final fixture in the national school's cup in the afternoon. The leadership group for our school was desperate for the team to do well, with the winning school receiving £25,000 in prize money. Before the fight, Connor had already been given a lunchtime detention for not doing his homework, and so if Mr Greasley gave him another one, he would have been given an afterschool detention, meaning that he would have to miss the semi-final. So, it's not hard to see why he didn't want to give Connor a detention. I could be wrong here, but I was a bit suspicious about the whole scenario.

The way in which the situation unfolded was difficult for me to swallow. I was incredibly upset at how unfair Mr Greasley had been. To make things worse, the detention that I got from Mr Greasley was my second in the same day, meaning that I was going to have to stay in school at the end of the day for an afterschool detention. Being given an afterschool detention on this day of all days was a huge disappointment, as it meant that I would have to get the "late bus", as my parents would not be able to pick me up (because of their conference).

Although £25,000 is a lot of money (which could be spent on trying to improve the school), by being unfair and not treating students equally, the school is setting a dangerous precedent. Personally, I think that it is more important for our school to have moral values that are respected by the teachers than to win a rugby tournament. After musing over my disappointments, I headed over to the first aid room to have a check-up.

CHAPTER 4

Back on track

So, because of the injuries that I sustained in my fight with Connor, I ended up missing my science class (which was the third lesson of the day). Science is probably one of my favourite lessons during the week, and so to miss it was very disappointing. While the school nurse, Miss Jennings, was cleaning up and bandaging the battle wound that had surfaced on my face, she asked me about how I got injured. I basically told her the ins-and-outs of everything that had happened, and she was shocked when I told her that Connor didn't get punished for punching me in the face. She then said that she would "have a word" with the principle, as she thought that it wouldn't be right for me to stay after school for a detention after everything that I had been through.

Once I had been bandaged up, Miss Jennings marched over to the principal's office, while I went to the Languages Block for my French lesson. I really was not looking forward to this lesson, as I felt incredibly sleepy, and on my way there I nearly walked straight into a door. Thankfully though, someone was there to hold open the door for me. I then arrived outside the classroom 5 minutes early. It was awkward waiting outside the classroom in this particular circumstance, as pretty much everyone who walked past me either stared at me inquisitively, or asked a load of questions about my fight with Connor. I was surprised as the sheer amount of people who seemingly knew about the fight as well. Although the situation was somewhat awkward, I did get a buzz out of the attention that I received, as most people knew who I was and wanted to talk to me. However at the same time I was a bit embarrassed that I was known around school as the guy who got beaten up by Connor.

Everyone else who was in my French class soon arrived, and as most of them were frantically trying to complete their homework moments before the lesson was due to start, few people from my class payed much attention me. I was extremely tired, and I really wasn't looking forward to an hour of French, especially as I'm not going to be taking it for my GCSE's.

As a class, we waited in the corridor for about 10 minutes before our teacher finally arrived. We were all really surprised when we saw that we were going to be having one of the supply teachers, Mr Pickett (especially as our usual French teacher, Mrs Perrins, supposedly hadn't missed a day of work for 12 years). Out of all of the supply teachers, Mr Pickett is definitely the most popular, and when he arrived everyone cheered and chanted his name as he walked down the corridor.

Once I knew that Mrs Perrins wasn't going to be teaching us, I saw a timely opportunity for me to sit back, relax, and regain some energy for the afternoon. I definitely wouldn't have been able to do this if Mrs Perrins was teaching, as she somehow notices everything that happens in her classes, while she's also notorious for being very strict. This was evident during my first lesson with her at the start of the academic year, as when she was writing on the board at the beginning of this lesson, I tossed a paper ball into the bin from the back of the classroom. It was an inch-perfect execution, landing directly into the bin without making too much noise. Yet, when everyone was leaving at the end of that lesson, out of the blue she told me to stay behind for throwing paper, and then sent me away with a detention. I was stunned.

Anyway, in terms of my lesson with Mr Pickett, I may have relaxed a bit too much, as I somehow managed to doze off within the first 5 minutes of the lesson. I don't think that anybody really noticed, as I ended up sleeping through the whole lesson (it probably helped that I was sat at the back of the class as well). In fact, I reckon that I would have slept through lunch as well if it wasn't for Vernon waking me up. At first, I was disappointed at being woken up from such a glorious nap, but after looking around and realising that everyone had gone to lunch, my mood quickly changed.

Vernon and I then headed to the dining room to get some lunch. To our dismay, we arrived to an extremely long queue. I really didn't feel like waiting in the queue, so instead we decided to go to L6, and buy our lunch a bit later instead. L6 is Mr Potts' classroom, and it's located on the first floor of the language block. It's one of the few non-IT classrooms with computers in, and kindly, he allows pupils to use his classroom at breaktime and lunch to hang out and use the computers. However, if you make too much noise he gets really annoyed and makes you leave. There's also a slight stigma attached to the room, as if someone uses L6 during breaktime and lunch, some kids label them as a 'sweaty gamer', even if they don't go in there to play games!

Anyway, spending time with Vernon on the computers is always an interesting and educational experience, as he is quite literally a computer whizz. When he's older, Vernon wants to be an inventor who is always looking for new ways to change the world in a way that adds value to other people's lives. I respect the hustle. So, when we went up to L6, we decided to spend a short amount of time looking at some coding for his upcoming invention, a computer-controlled fold-up bike. From what I saw, the bike, which was officially named "Verntron", certainly had something special about it, and this wasn't surprising considering that Vernon had been working on it for over 5 years.

After we had looked at Vernon's upcoming project, we spent a few minutes scrolling through our social media feeds, as Vernon has somehow found a way to bypass the school internet filters. Surprisingly, both of our feeds were filled with videos of the fight that I had with Connor, one of which had been viewed 15,000 times.

As the fight had been filmed from many different angles, there was clear evidence that Connor had lied to Mr Greasley about what had happened. Once I had rewatched several of the video clips, I asked Vernon if I could use his phone to show Mr Greasley the clips. We recognised that the phone would probably get confiscated, yet thankfully,

Vernon was willing to 'take one for the team' and let me use it.

We then raced over to the dining room, and arrived just as Mr Greasley was about to leave. He looked slightly startled when I told him that I had a video to show him, and at first, he refused to watch one of the videos as he said that he had an important meeting to attend. However, after I told him that the clip was really short, he reluctantly agreed to watch it. Due to the manner of my entrance into the dining hall, I had caught the attention of most people who were still in there eating their lunch, and at this point, all of the staff who were eating with Mr Greasley (and some other pupils) had eagerly gathered around Vernon's phone to watch the action unfold.

When the video had finished, Mr Greasley swiftly apologised to me, and immediately revoked the afterschool detention that I had been given, while he also said that Connor would have a detention. At first, he was reluctant to do this, but after pressure from the other teachers who had also watched the video, he quickly caved in. Although we were happy that I no longer had an afterschool attention, it was slightly disappointing that Vernon had his phone confiscated as a result, yet as he was allowed to retrieve it at the end of the day, it didn't really matter too much.

Shortly after we had sorted things out with Mr Greasley, we noticed that there was no longer a queue for food. I was looking forward to sinking my teeth into a spicy sausage, but due to its striking popularity amongst my fellow pupils, I had to settle for a bolognaise pasta pot instead.

We then proceeded towards the school field to play some football. As I approached one of the football pitches, I noticed that Connor was playing, and since I thought that it would be best for both of us if we let things cool down, I decided to play a bit of basketball instead. I'm not the best at basketball, but I certainly enjoyed doing something different. Barry, one of the basketball enthusiasts, even gave me a few tips on how to improve my three-point throws, which was pretty cool. I then faced Barry in a game of 1v1, which I managed to win by 1 point. The game ended dramatically as well, with me releasing the ball for an attempt at a three-pointer, nanoseconds before the school bell rang to signal the end of lunch. The ball then swished through the hoop, giving me an unexpected victory. Splash.

As Barry and I were in the same tutor group, we both headed towards our tutor room in the Humanities Block together. We soon had to pick up the pace, as our classroom was on the other side of the school to where the basketball hoop was. The only noise that could be heard was that of our shoes clattering against the floor as we closed in on our destination point.

We were soon 25 ft. from the door to our classroom, when something caught my eye behind one of the rubbish bins. At first, I thought that it was a cereal bar, but after having another glance I realised that it was a £20 note. I was tempted to pick the note up and keep it myself, however Barry encouraged me to hand it in as he pointed out that the person who had undoubtedly lost it would probably need it for something important, like a train ticket home. This was especially hard to do, as I only needed another £15 for a new phone that I had been saving up for. Although it was difficult, it did feel good to hand the money in. I was even told that I had a chance of keeping the money if it hadn't been claimed by the end of the year.

So, once I had handed the money into my tutor, Miss Penn, I sat down and got a good book out to read, as on Thursdays in tutor group, everyone in the school has to participate in a session of ERIC (which stands for "Everyone reading in Class"). It basically means that we have to read in silence for the duration of tutor. As I'm not really an avid reader, I usually have to ask Miss Penn if I can borrow one of her history magazines to read. I find them extremely boring, and it has definitely motivated me to try and find a good fiction book to read. It'll certainly make the time pass more quickly.

The bell soon rang meaning that I was finally allowed to leave for the last lesson of the day. This was Maths. As I was exhausted, I was kind of glad that Maths was going to be my last lesson for the day, as it's quite easy to sit through the lesson without properly engaging. I guess it's because of the lesson format, as our teacher, Mrs Drury, only briefly teaches us for 5 minutes at the beginning of the lesson, and 5 minutes at the end. For the middle 50 minutes in-between, we get given a set of questions to work through. During the middle part of the class, Mrs Drury goes around the class helping pupils, yet she primarily focuses on the pupils who are struggling near the bottom end of the class (in terms of grades). This means that unless I put my hand up, asking for Mrs Drury to help me, it's relatively easy to disengage and relax. So, all in all I was quietly pleased that Maths was the last lesson of the day for me.

After tutor, I walked over to the Maths Block for my last lesson. As I entered Mrs Drury's classroom, I was met with an unpleasant surprise when I discovered that the whole class was going to be doing a Maths test. At my school, it seems that everyone approaches these tests too seriously, especially when we regularly have one every half term (every 6 weeks on average). I guess that people probably get stressed over them due to the fear of moving down a set.

I always want to fulfil my potential when I do these tests, but when it comes to revising, I just don't have the energy or motivation to regularly engage myself in it. You see, every day I have to wake up early in the morning for the train to school. I then have to sit through 5 lessons a day, regularly learning about subjects that disinterest me. As a result, I'm usually exhausted by the time I arrive home.

Anyway, because I wanted the test to be over as soon as possible, I rushed through the questions as quickly as possible. In fact, I had gone so quickly through the test paper that I had managed to answer all of the questions with half-an-hour to spare. Once I had finished, I put my hand up to let the teacher know as I thought that I would then be able to go home early.

However, she said that I still had to wait until the end of the test before I was allowed to leave. I then checked over my answers several times, and once I had made a few changes, I looked at the clock and there were still 20 minutes left. In an attempt to quench my boredom, I started to build a pen tower using some spare pens that I had in my pencil case.

Unfortunately, as I was busy towering the pens on top of each other, ink from one of the pens began to squirt out onto my paper.

This was a disaster, as it made the first page of my exam paper unreadable. I knew that I would be in danger of failing if I lost all of my marks that were on the first page! At this point a level of panic began to settle in, and so without properly thinking things through, I quickly got a tissue out of my pocket and scrubbed the front page of the paper to try and wipe the ink away, contrarily causing the ink to become embedded in the paper. My unfortunate meltdown caught the attention of Mrs Drury, who simply gave me another test paper, once she had seen the state of my test paper.

I was momentarily relieved when I got a new sheet, as I could just copy the answers from my ruined sheet. However, some of my answers on the old sheet were unreadable from the ink spillage. When I answered one of these questions differently to the first time, I then began to grow anxious, as I wasn't sure which answer was actually the correct one. In the end, I went with the second answer, as I remember that I rushed through the questions when I first attempted this particular set of questions. Seconds after I fully completed the test, the school bell rang to signal the end of the day. I then wrote my name on the top of my new test sheet, before calmly walking out the door, and towards the main reception to retrieve my phone (and also see if anyone had claimed the £20 note which I had handed in).

When I retrieved my phone, I was glad to hear that someone called Gerald had claimed the money. He was in my Geography class, and it turns out he needed the money to pay for the geography field trip to Renchford Forest (which was on the following day). I'm happy that I handed it in, as the annual field trip to Renchford Forest is an important part of an assessment that significantly contributes to the end-of-year Geography grades for Year 9 students.

Unfortunately, when I attempted to check the time on my phone I quickly discovered that it didn't have any battery power left. This was very annoying, yet I was still full of excitement about the evening at home that I had planned. I soon met up with Ricky and Vernon, before the three of us walked over to the train station together.

CHAPTER 5

Fire

We soon arrived at the train station, ready to board
the train to Kettleston. We still had a few minutes
before the train was set to leave, and as there weren't
many snacks for us at my house, we decided to get
some extra supplies from Salltons (a supermarket near
the train station). In total, the cost of our food came to
£4.47. It seemed like a lot, but we did get a decent
half-price deal on the Choco rice and cheese puffs.
Although we were quite happy with what we bought
from Salltons, when we came to leave the shop and
looked at the time, we were in shock - we hadn't
missed the train for definite, but we would need to
run to have a chance of catching it. Whoops. I think
that most of the wasted time was spent when Ricky
couldn't decide whether to get cheese puffs or cheese
curls. Also, we had to wait in a queue for longer than

we would have liked because the person in front of us didn't know how to use the self-checkout machine.

After our trip to Salltons, we got to the ticket booth with 2 minutes to spare before the train was scheduled to leave. I went to get the train ticket, but as the tickets had gone up by 10p from £5.50 to £5.60 without me knowing, I was 7p short. I should I have bought a return ticket in the morning for £7.50, but the reason I didn't, was because I didn't want to break into my ten-pound note. I really liked this ten-pound note because it was a new plastic one that had recently been released into circulation, and so I figured that I would have been the only person at my school that had one.

I thought that it would have been cool to show the note to everyone in my tutor group, because before the first lesson of the day, it can be really boring sometimes, especially as I don't really have anything in common with anyone else the tutor group (apart from Barry). I was hoping that tenner would give me something to talk about. Ironically, I didn't get a proper chance to show everyone, as in the morning I simply forgot, and in the afternoon we had to read in silence for all of tutor.

So, I was a bit annoyed that we overspent in the shops, and I did think about returning some of the items. But unfortunately, Ricky had thrown the receipt away. I still only needed 7p, so I wasn't too concerned about the situation. I then asked Vernon and Ricky for some financial support. Vernon had a 5p coin, while Ricky had a 1p coin, meaning that we were only 1p short. Unbelievable! I then looked at the time - there was only 57 seconds remaining before the train left the station. Out of desperation, I asked the man at the ticket booth if he would lend me 1p.

I thought that he would surely just let me have a ticket, even if he didn't have any change on him, but unexpectedly, he refused to help me as he said that he was the guy who I jumped when I got Roger Jenkins shirt back in 2012. He was still upset at the whole situation, as apparently I "stole" the shirt off him, as he argues that Jenkins was aiming to give it to him when he threw the shirt into the crowd. I was lost for words - I guess that I was just so shocked that this guy still recognised me after 6 years! The clock was still ticking, and as I kind of felt sorry for the guy, I decided to offer him my Jenkins jumper. Yet, he didn't believe me that it was actually a jumper that once belonged to Jenkins. I guess he thought that I was trying to trick him.

As each second got swallowed up by the unstoppable arrow of time, more and more ideas of what to do raced through my head like a racing car that was driving through the last corner of an intense race. Ricky and Vernon already had their tickets, and they weren't helping me much. However, they could see that I was anxious, so Vernon began to do a crazy dance in an attempt to cheer me up. Astonishingly, a passer-by tossed a coin in Vernon's direction. I guess he thought that it was a good dance, and that he was doing it for money. I couldn't believe it. We had enough money to buy the ticket. With 12 seconds left I bought my ticket. Once I had my ticket, the three of us then ran towards the train, and just as we were about to enter through the door, it shut on us. I couldn't believe it.

While Ricky and I had been stunned into silence at what had just happened, Vernon calmly got something out of his bag. It was the Verntron Bike! Vernon suggested that the three of us should ride on it to catch up to the train. As the Verntron still had to pass two more weeks of scheduled testing until it was ready for use, Vernon told us that there was a slight risk that the bike could blow up if we used it.

As the trains in England travel at about 60mph, Vernon suggested that we would be able to catch up to the train, as the Verntron has a top speed of 90mph. The clock was ticking. Vernon insisted that the bike would probably pass all of the safety tests and that we should risk using it. Usually, I would say no to

Vernon, but for some reason I decided to go ahead with Vernon's suggestion. Ricky then reluctantly agreed as well.

The three of us then scrambled onto the motorbike, before zooming off to catch the train. Because we were headed towards a double railway track, Vernon steered the bike to go in-between the two tracks, as it was a relatively flatter surface for us to ride on. The ride was really bumpy however, and as we weren't riding on a flat tarmac road, it was harder for the Verntron to get up to speed.

Fortunately, Vernon had installed a special turbo boost feature into the motorbike, which enabled it to travel at a top speed of 180mph when activated. This feature could only be controlled via the 'Verntron' app that Vernon had created, and it only lasted for 20 seconds. Prior to this ride, the fastest that I had ever gone in a vehicle was about 70mph on the motorway, so when Vernon actually decided to initiate the turbo boost, the sheer speed of the bike came as a shock to me, almost causing me to pass out. In fact, we entered into a dangerous situation on so many different levels, as we went so fast that we actually ended up overtaking the train!

As we overtook the train, Vernon tried to slow down, but because the turbo boost couldn't be cancelled once it was initiated, we were unable to properly slow down. Vernon then panicked, as it looked as if we were going to crash into a post. He then slammed on the breaks, and veered us to the side, momentarily sliding us into the rails as an oncoming train was approaching. Fortunately, Vernon managed to steer us off the rails, just before one of the oncoming trains went past. However, we continued to travel at a fast pace, heading straight towards a nearby forest. We then entered the forest, narrowly avoiding a few trees, but out of nowhere, we found ourselves driving towards a mighty oak. For a moment, it looked like we were definitely going to crash. Yet, all three of us planted our feet into the ground, hoping to slow the bike down. It wasn't going to be enough though, so instinctively, I grabbed one of the bike's handlebars, and aggressively steered it to the side. We avoided the tree, but the three of us didn't exactly come to a comfortable halt, as we ended up rolling over and skidding across the floor. Although my trousers had been shredded, and my arms and legs had many cuts and bruises, I was sure that the three of us would have come off worse if we had crashed into the oak tree. Vernon and Ricky also had a few cuts, but they both agreed that I did the right thing.

I then tried to find my bearings, but after looking around for a few seconds, it soon came to my attention that I had no idea where we were. We were simply in the middle of a massive forest that was unknown to the three of us. Vernon and Ricky tried to use their phones to find our location, but unfortunately, neither of them could get a signal. We were well and truly lost. Yet, Vernon and I were soon more optimistic when we remembered that Ricky was in the boy scouts. Although Ricky didn't seem very confident about navigating us home, after some encouragement from Vernon and I, he hesitantly agreed to take charge of the situation.

Ricky then explained to us that he could approximately calculate our location from looking at the position of the sun, and from his calculations, the journey to my house would take no longer than 15 minutes (12 minutes through the woods, and 3 minutes zooming along the roads at 60mph). However, after 28 minutes we were still in the woods, and it felt like we were walking around in circles. As time went on, I gradually began to lose confidence in Ricky's navigation skills.

I asked Ricky whether he actually knew where we were going, and he insisted that he knew where we were going. We then rolled into a discussion about his experiences in the boy scouts, and it turned out that he had managed to earn every single badge apart from one: the navigation badge. Vernon and I were left disappointed. As each second ticked by, it seemed that our hopes of playing computer games at my house in the evening were slowly melting away, like a tub of ice cream that has been left outside on a hot summer's day. I felt like we were more lost than we had been before.

A huge amount of energy had seemingly been sapped out of me, with every step feeling as if I was walking through a room of treacle. With the three of us getting more and more tired as the day grew older, Ricky suggested that we use the Verntron. Originally I was against this, but when Vernon agreed with Ricky, I was outnumbered two-to one.

So, we gradually eased our way through the forest on the Verntron, but unexpectedly, it broke down. The situation soon turned serious though, as the bike blew up into flames. Fortunately, we were all a safe distance from the bike when it exploded, however, Vernon nearly got seriously injured as the bike blew up just moments before he was going to approach it.

Apparently, a malfunction with the engine had occurred, causing an explosion. Also, we discovered that we had run out of fuel. This was because the petrol tank had a leakage from when we skidded to avoid crashing into the oak tree. A trail of petrol that had formed from a leak in the bike while it was being dragged along by Vernon suddenly caught fire. Consequently, much of the surrounding vegetation began to light up in flames. Wisps of fear began to whirl about, whilst a heavy atmosphere of dread began to emerge. We were lost, with no phone signal, no compass, no map, no money, and three expired train tickets. The plan for the games night was seemingly starting to go up in flames.

The fire was getting bigger and bigger, and before we knew it, we were beginning to get engulfed by the emerging furnace. However, out of the corner of my eye, I noticed a cave on top of a small ledge, about 10 ft. up from the ground. Whilst trying to shield ourselves from the furnace's flickering flames, I alerted Ricky and Vernon to the cave. Running as fast as we could, we rushed over to the bottom of the ledge. After many attempts to climb onto the ledge, it was clear to us that we faced a monumental challenge to survive the situation that we found ourselves in. The increasing heat from the fire only made the circumstance more difficult for us to endure. For a moment, I literally thought that this day could have been my last on planet earth. So, while eating some of the marshmallows that we had bought from Salltons, I attempted to come up with an escape strategy.

After enjoying some delicious marshmallows, I asked Vernon and Ricky to hold their hands out for me to run onto, before making a giant leap for the ledge. I tried and I failed. I was slumped against a rock feeling depressed, when I felt something land on my head. It was as if someone had just thrown down a rope. I turned around and that was exactly what had happened. Out of pure instinct, I alerted Ricky and Vernon before they could get swallowed up by the approaching flames. We then set out to climb up the rope as quickly as possible. As Vernon and I were climbing, we were so focused on escaping the flames that we didn't notice Ricky lying on the ground, coughing while his trousers were also on fire. I was near the top, but almost intuitively, I hastily climbed down to help him, unfortunately spraining my ankle as a result of an awkward landing.

When I got down to Ricky, I was alarmed when I noticed that the tip of his trousers had caught fire. I quickly stripped off Ricky's trousers, and tied his hands to the rope, enabling Vernon to pull him up. Once Ricky was safely up, Vernon then let the rope down, allowing me to climb to the top.

Once I got up, I saw that there was a girl with Vernon. Her name was Millie, and she was the person who threw the rope down for us. After introducing myself to her, she told us that she was an explorer looking for some lost treasure. I then started to chuckle as I thought that she was joking, but after seeing the expression on her face, I got the impression that she was actually being serious, however, I still wasn't convinced.

This was definitely awkward for me. The situation got even more uncomfortable when Ricky asked us if we knew where his phone was. At first, I told him that I didn't have a clue where it was, but after realising that I had probably left it behind in the fire with his trousers, I reluctantly told him where it probably was.

Ricky, Vernon, and I were planning on staying in the cave to figure out what to do. However, Millie invited us to join her on her quest. As we only had one other option of staying where we were, the three of us decided to go with her. This definitely felt like the best decision at the time, especially considering that the fire was only getting bigger and more dangerous. I was even hoping that the fire wouldn't get out of control and spread to a local neighbourhood.

While I was thinking about all of this, we all heard the noise of the fire brigade turning up. I did think about turning back to wait for them to save us, however, I also didn't want to 'turn myself in', as I thought that all of us could get into big trouble if we were known to have started the fire. I remembered that Millie was with us and that she could easily tell everyone about us. I still didn't fully trust Millie at this point, as she didn't go to my school and I still barely knew her.

I was going to persuade her not to tell anybody that we started the fire. But I then remembered something significant, just as I was about to talk to her – she had no way of fully knowing that we were responsible for the fire. However, as I wasn't fully convinced, I asked her if she knew who started the fire, and after she said that she had no idea, I was a lot more relieved. I then proceeded to ask about why she was in the middle of a mysterious forest on her own, as I still didn't think that she was actually serious about looking for treasure. She then pulled a treasure map out of her backpack, before showing it to me.

Millie told me that she had been on a quest all over Wiltshire and Berkshire, looking for the clues to the treasure for about 6 months. Apparently, she had found 5 of them, meaning that she only needed 2 more (as she needed to find 7 clues). She then went on to explain that there was some gold bars that had been hidden by an old man who had mysteriously died in a manor house in 2017. Just before he died, he hid his gold in a secret location and several clues connected to it dotted in and around the two neighbouring counties of Wiltshire and Berkshire. Although Millie seemed incredibly enthusiastic about her quest, she did express feelings of anxiety, as there was also another set of clues for the first 5 out of the 7, meaning that if someone had found the other original note leading to the other set of clues, either the treasure would have already been found, or she would be in an active race for the 6th clue with another person (there was only one set of clues for the last 2)!

After hearing about this, I was really unsure about getting involved, as the whole thing sounded a bit sketchy to me, while I was also curious as to how Millie came to hear about the treasure. She then said that as she was a natural explorer, she saw the old abandoned manor after school one day, before going inside to explore it. She was walking through the downstairs corridor and fell through the floorboards into a secret underground room. While she was inside this room, she found a mile-long tunnel that led to a secret chamber. The chamber was completely empty, apart from an unlocked treasure chest that merely contained a handwritten note, outlining the first clue.

I was eager to hear more of the story from Millie, but after turning around and seeing that the firefighters were spraying water everywhere, I realised that it would not be long before they noticed the four of us if we didn't make a bold move from the cave entrance. Suddenly, we saw one of the firemen running towards us. As the visibility was much clearer, it was likely that he had spotted us. I really didn't want us to be caught, so without a moment for us to lose, we ran into the tunnel without stopping. The tunnel was a lot darker than we had expected, and as we journeyed through, the darkness got more intense.

All of a sudden, we abruptly came across a very sharp drop. Millie, Ricky and I managed to stop in time. Unfortunately though, Vernon wasn't paying much attention and crashed into the three of us, sending us all downwards. At first, it was a 90-degree vertical drop downwards. Yet thankfully, it wasn't long before the surface below us flattened out into a slope meaning that instead of falling in mid-air, we were able to roll. However, this was still a frightening experience as we had no idea where we were rolling to.

We soon found ourselves gliding downwards through mid-air again. I thought that I was going to plunge into the ground and get seriously injured. SPLASH!

Abruptly, all four of us had dropped into a pool of cold water. The fact that the water was cold was very refreshing due to all of the heat that I had previously experienced. Although the light was very dim, my eyes adapted quickly and fortunately, I was able to see everyone. We were all sculling water, yet the realisation that we couldn't scull water forever soon kicked in – we needed to find somewhere to rest. Things soon became more frightening when I looked over at Vernon, who seemed to be struggling to keep his head above the water. Millie, Ricky, and I rapidly swam over to help, but we knew that we needed to find somewhere to rest quickly. I frantically looked around for somewhere to rest, but there wasn't an obvious place for us to go, so I stuck my head underwater and desperately hoped for an opening of some sort underwater. It was incredibly difficult for me to adjust my eyes to the water, especially considering that I'm used to wearing goggles. Nevertheless, it was a lot easier than I thought it would be.

The water was quite clear, and just as I was about to run out of breath, I noticed a gleam of light coming out of an entrance to an underwater tunnel. As I came back up I went to tell everyone about the tunnel. Thankfully, they had found a ledge, yet the difficult part would be for us to climb it. When I mentioned to everyone that I had potentially found an underwater tunnel, Mille got really excited. She then told us that an underwater tunnel was related to the clue that she had found for her treasure hunt thing. Although I still had some doubts about the legitimacy of the whole treasure hunt thing, as time went by I was beginning to become more and more convinced that Millie was actually onto something.

We then began to debate whether we should try and find a way out of the cave by going back up, or continue down into the underwater tunnel. Ricky said that it was too risky to go underwater, as he argued that the tunnel could go on forever, meaning that we would drown. He then said that we should try climbing back up. I actually thought that this was a good idea. Millie was really against this as she was desperate to find her treasure. We ended up doing a vote. It was 3 votes to 1 in favour of us climbing back up. However, Millie was so determined to find the treasure that she ended up swimming towards the underwater tunnel regardless.

So at this point, I really didn't have much energy left, and it was getting harder for us to keep Vernon up above the water. We swam to the edge of the pool of water, directly below the ledge that we had found. There were some rock panels sticking out and the experience was similar to that of a climbing wall, except that the rocks were very slippery and also none of us had a harness. In fact, it was a lot more difficult than I had first presumed. I was thinking that I should have gone into the underwater tunnel with Millie. After 7 attempts, we all made it onto the small ledge about 11 ft. up from the water. This was huge for us as it gave us a useful resting point. Our feeling of triumph soon came to an abrupt end when we looked directly upwards, realising that we still had another 50 ft. to climb, and by the looks of it, there weren't any more ledges that we could rest on.

After getting up from a brief 5-minute power nap, I looked upwards and noticed someone, quickly realising that it was the fireman who I had seen outside. He must have followed us, and I was flabbergasted that he was still after us.

Without hesitation, the fireman then began to climb down like a ninja, and so without a moment to lose, I quickly alerted Vernon and Ricky of the fireman's presence. The way that he climbed downwards at such a fast and smooth rate was really impressive. After alerting Vernon and Ricky, the three of us desperately tried to conjure up an exit strategy. Ricky said that we should turn ourselves in, as he said that we would at least be able to get home safely. However, Vernon thought that this could be risky, as he emphasised that there was a possibility that the fireman could be a psycho.

We were torn between what we should do. Suddenly, the fireman dropped down, landing behind us. He then headed straight for Vernon, who quickly moved before the fireman could grab him. Unfortunately, Vernon then lost his balance, causing him to fall off the ledge and into the water.

Vernon looked like he was in trouble. The fireman then tried to grab me, and as a reflex reaction, I swiftly dived into the waters below. SPLASH. I'm sure that I made the right decision as Vernon was really struggling to keep his head above the water. Fortunately, I managed to help him keep afloat by holding onto him. But, I then recollected that Ricky was still on the ledge, sleeping.

Back on the ledge, Ricky had just been awoken by the splash. The fireman hadn't noticed him until he awoke, and from seeing the fireman, Ricky gasped with shock as he was right by the man we were meant to be running away from. The fireman then charged towards Ricky, who then proceeded to try and roll over the edge, into the water. Just as Ricky was about to roll over, the fireman dived and grabbed a hold of Ricky's shirt. Ricky was perilously hanging from the edge. The fireman was desperately trying it pull him up. Ricky then frantically unbuttoned his shirt, causing him to fly into the water like a professional diver. He actually looked like one as well, as he was just wearing his pants. Splosh! Although the initial 'dive' through the air looked good, the execution wasn't great.

At this point, we decided that our best option was to try and find Millie. I then looked upwards towards the fireman, and immediately I got the impression that he was readying himself for a dive into the water. I then took a deep breath, before going underwater to see if I could locate the tunnel again, and straight away I was able to find it. Bravely, the three of us then got ready to try and execute our plan. The plan was to swim as fast as we could into the tunnel (Vernon would have to grab onto Ricky and I), and if we didn't think that we could hold our breath for long enough, we decided that we would swim back to turn ourselves in.

We then looked up, and as we saw that the fireman was about to jump in after us, the three of us dunked our heads underwater, and swam as fast as we could towards the underwater tunnel. When we made it into the underwater tunnel, it was noticeably brighter. We had been swimming for about 5 metres through the tunnel, before the tunnel began to curve upwards. A strong current then took hold of us rapidly channelling us all upwards. At this point, we didn't really have to do any swimming due to the ferocity of the current. I was beginning to get desperate for some air and I honestly thought that I was on the verge of drowning. WHOOSH! We were spurted out and landed in another rocky cave-like area, although this time there was a small opening at the top. It was great to finally be able to see some daylight.

CHAPTER 6

Butch

I had a pretty rough landing, with my hip especially hurting after I had landed on it. It felt like I had just been shot out of a Whales' blowhole. I looked to see if Vernon and Ricky were okay – they seemed fine which was good. We looked at where we had entered from, and it looked just like a fountain that was continually spraying out water. One thing was for sure though - we couldn't go back from where we came, as the current was definitely too strong for us to swim against.

After getting up, I sat up against a big rock to try and recover. Vernon then came over to me saying that the three of us should set a trap for the fireman, as he argued that we would anxiously be looking over our shoulders for the rest of the day if we didn't. I then called Ricky over to see if he had any ideas as to what we could do for this. He suggested that we should surprise the fireman by jumping on him unexpectedly, forming a big pile on, before pinning him down and tying him up. However, I was partially against this, as we didn't have any rope to tie the fireman up with (as Millie took it with her).

We quickly realised that we probably didn't have long before the fireman popped up. We were running out of time and unsure of what to. So, we decided to look for a place to hide, hoping that the fireman would walk past us, get bored, and go home. While looking for a place to hide, I managed to find a small gap between two rocks that had been wedged together. I then called over Ricky and Vernon to show them. Although the gap was small, it was big enough for the three of us to fit in without being seen. However, once we had crawled in, we were amazed to discover that the gap was an entrance to another area. It wasn't as big as the cave we were in before (it was about the same size as an average-sized bedroom). In the same instant, we saw Millie scraping the walls with a spoon. I presumed that she was looking for the treasure. It was good to know that she was okay, and when she noticed us, she seemed happy to see us. Immediately, we got into a conversation about her treasure quest, and it turned out that we had found the exact location of the next clue according to her clue sheet, yet Millie was still struggling to find the clue. I suggested that there may be some sort of special button that's meant to be pressed, but after offering this piece of advice, she said that I had been watching too many films.

Suddenly, we heard footsteps coming from the main cave. We assumed that it was the fireman, and so I told Millie that our plan to catch him would probably work now that we had her rope. She agreed to this and from here, our plan was to jump on the fireman, hopefully giving Millie an opportunity to tie his legs together. This would be important for us, as once the fireman had his legs tied together, we knew that he wouldn't be able to run after us. However, I alternatively suggested that it would be better if we pinned him facedown, then tie his hands behind his back, as by doing this he wouldn't be able to attack. We all agreed on this. To make sure that the plan worked, we needed to set some sort of trap for the fireman to walk into. For this, we planned on getting Ricky to lie down on the floor, looking as if he was asleep. Hopefully, the fireman would then approach him, giving Vernon and I the opportunity to jump on him, while Mille tied him up.

We were right; the footsteps belonged to the fireman. When the fireman had his back turned, Ricky snuck out into the opening to lie-down on the floor. Unfortunately though, the fireman perceived that one of us was going to come out of the opening, and caught Ricky in his midst. Ricky screamed the signal that something was going wrong (which was woof – like a dog). The fireman was probably thinking that Ricky had gone barking mad, but this was just the signal for Plan B. Plan B was for all of us to come out of the opening as fast as possible to overpower the fireman. We certainly caught him off guard as he was taken aback by the sheer force that had been thrown at him. The plan worked, with us managing to pin him down and tie him up.

Once we had captured the fireman, we were really unsure as to what to do. However, when Millie saw who the fireman was from close up, she was shocked – it was her cousin, Butch. It turned out that Millie hadn't seen him for 5 years, which is why she didn't fully recognise him from a distance. She was not expecting to see him in England, as Butch and his family had been living in the USA for the past 5 years. Butch also said that he didn't recognise Millie at first either. After Millie asked for an explanation from Butch as to why he was in the forest, he openly explained to us that he was also on a quest for the treasure, and that he wasn't a fireman at all. Apparently, he found out about the treasure when he was helping to clean and clear out the house that the rich man used to live in. While Butch was having a break from lifting old heavy furniture, he found a note consisting of a clue and map inside an old book that he had found on a bookshelf in the library area of the house.

For Butch, this whole experience in England came about from a summer of volunteering in Europe during the summer of 2017. He came over to England for the main part of his European placement, and during this time he spent a week in Berkshire helping to tidy up the premises that the rich man had been living in. After finding the first clue, Butch said that he spent the rest of his time in England (during the summer of 2017) on a quest to find as many of the clues as he could. He managed to find 5 of the clues before travelling back to the USA for school. He then said that because his family were in England for a week on a short holiday in the countryside, it was a prime opportunity for him to continue his quest.

This meant that Butch was on the other trail for the treasure that Millie had previously spoken about. Likewise, Butch was also aware that another separate trail of clues leading to the 6th clue also existed. Just to make sure that everything added up, I asked to have a look at Butch's clue, to see if the details of his 5th clue were the same as our 5th clue. He then told us that it was in one of his pockets with a map that he had drawn up. Following this, I reached into his pocket expecting to find a map, but instead my fingers got covered in sticky chewing gum. Butch apologised, remembering that the clue was in fact inside his helmet "to keep it dry". So, I unclipped his helmet, and behold there was a soggy piece of paper – it was a note that consisted of the clue and a detailed map. When getting it out, I had to be very careful not to rip it because of how soggy it was. I then put the note out in front of everyone. Although the note seemed to be exactly the same as Millie's, I was slightly confused as to why only one of Butch's clues was the same as the clues that were in Millie's set.

It seemed especially odd to me that both of the treasure trails had 5 different checkpoints, while the last 2 checkpoints were shared by both of the distinct trails. Butch then told us of a proposed theory of his that seemingly explained why the quest had been formulated in this way. Butch went on to say that he had read (or heard) that the rich man was born on the 5th February 1952 (meaning that his D.O.B read 5/2/52). From this, Butch told us that he believed that the rich man had cryptically implemented a key aspect of his personal identity into the underlying structure of how the clues fitted together for the quest (5 different checkpoints submerging into 2 single ones). In fact, the fifth clue even stated that there would be a potential race for the 6th clue, as it said only the bearer of the 6th clue would reach the last checkpoint.

As we didn't think that Butch would try any dirty tricks on us, we untied him and let him examine the map with us to see if he could help us identify where the next clue was. It also seemed reasonable to think that Butch was telling the truth. Butch then suggested that we would probably have a higher chance of finding the treasure if all of us worked together. Just before we were going to release Butch, we searched him for weapons, etc. as a precaution.

After we had untied Butch, we asked him about why he was dressed up in a fireman's costume, and why he seemingly chased after is. Coincidently, he just so happened to have been in the forest at the same time as Millie, and as she was looking at a piece of paper and going towards the same cave as he was, he presumed that they were both in the forest for the same reason. When the fire brigade came, he said that he snuck into the fire engine and 'borrowed' a firefighter's uniform, as he thought that we might get scared if he came over to us dressed in normal clothes (as he didn't recognise Millie from a distance).

Although we knew that the clue was in the area between the two rocks that had been wedged together, we still didn't know its exact whereabouts. Vernon said that he had once read a book about a group of treasure hunters who shone their map in direct sunlight to reveal extra pieces of information. I told Vernon that he needed to grow up, and that he was talking of fantasy make-believe baloney. However, Millie said that Vernon might have a point, before suggesting that we look at the map under the sunlight, which was coming down from directly above the cave, to see if any other clues on the sheet would emerge.

Vernon was right! By holding the map under a light, certain contents of the map became increasingly clear, and amazingly a big X also became visible. Immediately, we figured out that it was extremely likely that this marked where the next clue was. The only problem we had was that we had to keep the map in the sunlight to see where the X was, as we couldn't take a picture of it using our phones (as they were all either broken from being underwater or out of battery (or lost)).

Millie and Butch paced back and forth between the map and the hidden-away area in order to get a sense of the surroundings. We soon had a general idea of the exact location of where the X was marked, which Millie had marked on the floor for us. All of us then entered into the small area (through the two rocks that had been wedged together), taking the map with us.

As the next clue was seemingly underground, we all assumed that we would have to do a lot of digging together, which would not be easy considering that we didn't have a spade or anything like that. The only thing we had that somewhat resembled a spade was a small teaspoon. Millie seemed to be really upset with how things had turned out, while I could tell that Butch was also trying to hide his disappointment. So, to try and help out, I splashed some water on the ground, hoping that it would be easier for us to scrape away at the ground. No one else seemed that enthusiastic about my idea, and so I ended up churning up the ground by myself. However, as my method seemed to be working, Butch came over to help.

Suddenly the floor gave way, and I found myself plunging downwards into an unknown dark chasm. Everyone else screamed in horror as I slipped out of sight. Butch desperately hung out his hand for me to grab. I grabbed hold of it, but unfortunately, I ended up pulling him down with me. CRASH! We ended up falling down 12 ft. onto a small crate.

I found myself in a strange state while I slowly started to recover from what had just befallen me. I was okay though, and as I got up I was relieved to see that Butch was also fine. The rest of the crew then called down to see if we were okay. They couldn't see us due to the sheer darkness of the hole that we found ourselves in. Although it wasn't pitch-black, we did have difficulty seeing each other.

I soon realised that we were probably very close to the next clue, as we fell down directly below the X that we had marked! We needed a torch though. I was sure that what we were looking for would have been in the crate which we fell on. I called up to the rest of the crew to tell them that I had found some sort of crate. Millie was then filled with excitement, before telling Butch and I to bring up anything that either of us could find. As we didn't have any torches, Butch and I had to trace our hands around the broken crate (and the ground) to see if we could find anything that might resemble the next clue. I then came across an envelope that was stuck to the bottom of the crate - I was certain that this was the clue.

Once I had notified everyone, Mille threw down her rope for Butch and I to climb back up, and regroup. As Butch and I both climbed back up, we could sense that Millie, Vernon, and Ricky were filled with enthusiasm. We huddled around, and I carefully opened the envelope. Inside was a yellow brown piece of paper that had been folded in half. I was sure that the old guy, who had written up the clues, had dipped the paper in some tea and burnt the edges to try and add an ancient look. I kind of understand this, as if the piece of paper was merely a typed-up piece of A4, it would definitely not have been as exciting for us. Nevertheless, it probably would've been better if it hadn't been dipped in tea (if it was), as technically this could be deemed as an attempt at manipulating reality. This was similar to the time when TV companies implemented artificial crowd noise into the official audio of an English cup game between Droitwich United and Westminster Warriors, back in 2015. The game was being played behind closed doors because of a breach in the league rules by Droitwich for using an ineligible player in a previous game. Apparently they had 'forgotten' that the player was suspended, but the fact that he was their best player did make me think otherwise.

Anyway, the piece of paper turned out to be another map. This time, it was one of Renchford Forest (not the forest that we were in). According to the maps, the new clue was located in a specific oak tree in the centre of the forest, with the five of us presuming that it was somewhere inside a small opening within the tree.

After thoroughly examining the map, we all soon came to the stark realisation that we needed to find a way out. After carefully looking around, it seemed as if we were going to be trapped. The only way that seemed remotely possible for us to find a way out, was to climb. About 25-30 ft. upwards from the ground was a very small opening. From this opening, the ceiling of the cave curved outwards, meaning that if we climbed upwards from one of the walls, we would soon find ourselves crawling upside down due to the smooth gradient change.

The only plan which we could devise was for one of us to climb up with the rope and squeeze through the opening, before finding something to tie the rope to. This would then enable the rest of us to climb up one-by-one. Out of the five of us, Ricky and Millie were the only ones who had any sort of climbing experience. Millie swiftly put herself forward to climb up first for us.

Along the sides of the cave, there were many rocks jutting that resembled that of a climbing wall. The only potential issue that we had with climbing was the danger of Millie coming across a loose rock and slipping. Although there was an element of risk attached to the challenging climb, Mille adamantly said that she would be able to do it with ease, especially as she had done "tougher climbs than this before". Her confidence was contagious, and I could sense that it gave the rest of us a sense of self-belief. As Millie began to climb up, the rest of us then stood directly below as a safety precaution.

Millie rapidly climbed up – she was like a ninja. However, she nearly fell down while she was trying to squeeze through the gap at the top of the cave. Once she had made it through, she got her rope and tied it to the nearest tree. Millie then let the rope down for us to climb, and it was definitely a lot harder to climb that I thought it was going to be at first.

The rope was continuously jolting while I climbed upwards, as I didn't have anything to lean against. I finally reached the top, and once I got through the cavern and into the open world again, I was filled with a great sense of relief. When I first came up, I immediately noticed that the sky had dimmed dramatically, while the emergence of a fresh breeze also helped me to cool down and reflect on the adventure that I had just been on. While Millie, Ricky, and I waited for Vernon and Butch to come up, I briefly rested on some nearby lush, green grass. I was caught in two minds at this point. I still wanted to go home and play computer games with my mates while I also wanted to explore the area that we were in, and hold discussions with everyone about getting to

Renchford Forest to find the treasure. I rested for a short while, waiting for everyone else to climb up.

CHAPTER 7

Momentum

Once everybody had come up, we sat down to discuss what to do next. We soon discovered that Ricky had actually been so bad at directing us, that instead of leading us to my house, he led us in the opposite direction to another county. We had somehow wandered into Berkshire, Millie and Butch's home county.

We were unsure of how to get back to my house. Butch said that he knew the way back to the place where he was staying from where we were and that he could drive us all to my house once we got to his car. We were only 10 minutes away from Butch's place, and the short trek to the apartment that his family were staying at was one of the best walks that I have ever experienced.

When we arrived at the apartment, Butch briefly let us inside to get a quick drink (while Ricky also went to get a change of clothes). Butch's parents both seemed really laid back, as when Butch said that he was going to drive us to my house, they both seemed to be fine with everything. We then headed over to Butch's car, which was parked in a nearby multi-storey car park.

When we got out of the lift, I immediately called shotgun. Unfortunately though, everyone else was apparently thinking alike, as I was the last to call shotgun. This was unfortunate, especially when taking into account the size of the car, as it was incredibly small. As I was the last to call 'shotgun', it meant that I was the one who had to sit in the middle seat of the car. Although at first this seemed like the worst option, I think that the side middle seats were worse or just on par with my seat, as Millie and Ricky (who were both sat next to me) had to have their knees up by their chin dues to the limited leg room. This didn't make the middle seat seem any more comfortable though, as my knees had to be as close together as possible, causing considerable discomfort.

Anyway, it was about 7:20 p.m. by the time we were all in the car, zooming off to my house. Butch had rented a very small car for his time in England and the fact that it had been installed with a hi-tech satnav, which tells the driver exactly how far away they are from the desired destination point, partly made up for the discomfort of the journey. Vernon typed in my address, and I was shocked when the satnav said that my house was 40 minutes away from where Butch was staying! WOW!

As Butch was a very fast driver, the estimated time of arrival steadily trickled away. While zooming down the motorway at a very high speed, Butch told all of us about his goal of becoming a racing car driver in the USA. He said that he was currently the top driver in a racing car academy for a big team and that he was hopeful of competing in professional races at speedways by the time he was 21. To be honest, I was surprised when he implied that he was younger than 21, as it turns out that he was only 17. At first, I wasn't sure whether or not to believe Butch, but...on this one, I decided to give him the benefit of the doubt, especially as his driving was pretty smooth. He then said that this was partly why he disguised himself as a fireman, as he said that he didn't want to be recognised as a famous racing driver while he was wandering through a forest on a treasure quest.

We soon approached my home county of Wiltshire, and as we went past my school, I knew that we weren't too far away from Kettleston. About 20 minutes after we entered into Wiltshire we arrived at my house. I then jumped out of the car and approached the front door, ready to unlock it. I unlocked the door and opened it, but as it opened, the burglar alarm suddenly went off in the house. This was a bit of a problem, as I didn't actually know what the code was to turn the alarm off. This had never happened to me before, as someone is usually in the house when I get home. I then realised that this probably meant that Katie wasn't in the house.

I honestly didn't know what to do. After trying to get through to my parents on the phone several times, the most tempting thing to do was to smash the alarm up, in the hope that it would stop making such a loud noise. However, I was sensible enough to realise that breaking the alarm system would probably result in me forking out all of my birthday and Christmas money combined to pay for a new one.

I then decided to have a go at guessing the code. For my first attempt, I entered in the digits for the year my family moved into the house, 2008. It didn't work.

This was not a nice situation to experience, with the alarm seemingly getting louder. However, Vernon quietly emerged from my kitchen with a screwdriver and calmly unscrewed the face off the alarm controls. He then did some twiddling and fiddling with some of the wires and managed to disable the alarm. I was relieved. After managing to alert half of the neighbourhood (who were all looking out of their windows at us), we locked the door and sat around the dining room table. I then went into the kitchen to put the kettle on, before going up to my room to put on a fresh change of clothes.

When I came back down, we had a meeting to discuss how we were going to get to Renchford Forest, which was on the Wiltshire-Berkshire border. Conveniently, Vernon, Ricky, and I had a Geography field trip to Renchford Forest the next day. We weren't sure how Millie and Butch could get there, as Millie was going to be in school all-day, while Butch said that he was going be in London with his parents. Out of curiosity, I asked Butch what he wanted to be if his hopes of a racing career didn't work out. He told us that he would try and work as an archaeologist for the British Archaeologist Society. I wasn't completely sure what an archaeologist does, and as I was too embarrassed to ask Butch, I went onto the internet to search about them. Apparently, they discover and examine old artefacts. It then made sense to me why Butch took the treasure quest so seriously. As someone who seemed to be interested in archaeology, he probably found the treasure hunt aspect of the clues to be interesting.

As Millie and Butch weren't able to get to the forest on Friday, Vernon, Ricky and I had the responsibility to look for the final clue ourselves. There wasn't really anything else to be discussed, meaning that it was time for us to finally play football on the MegaWay 5. We asked Mille and Butch if they wanted to stay, but I think that they were both quite exhausted, as they both politely rejected the offer and went back home to Berkshire.

We then played computer games until about 11 p.m. Katie came home at about 9 p.m. and sat with us, as she had been at a friend's house revising. The evening was starting to get a bit boring, with the three of us playing each other over and over again. Our records were pretty similar, with all of us winning two matches each.

To make things more interesting, we invited my next-door neighbour Jimmy over so that we could do a 2v2 match. He was happy to play (although his parents weren't keen on him staying over too late). For the 2v2 match, Jimmy and I were on the same team playing as Westminster Warriors, while Ricky and Vernon played as Nottingham Friday. We didn't actually realise this until we started playing, but this match was reminiscent of the first (and only) Westminster Warriors match that I had been to, when Roger Jenkins scored THAT goal. Jenkins was still the best Westminster player by a long way, and so for this reason, Jimmy and I built our team around him to suit his style of play. Nottingham weren't very good when I watched them play versus Westminster, but since then they have signed some quality players, improving dramatically. In fact, they nearly won the top division in 2017, and only lost out to the team that finished 1st on goal difference.

So, as we changed the settings to make the game a lot longer than the standard 10-minute matches that the game was designed for, there were a lot of goals. Unfortunately, Jimmy and I lost the game 8-5. I think that it was maybe because Jimmy was a bit 'rusty' compared to Ricky, Vernon, and I, as us three had already been playing the game for a while before Jimmy came. Although it was disappointing to lose, I still thoroughly enjoyed the match. For Jimmy and I, Roger Jenkins scored four goals, while Charlie Trundle also scored from outside the box. Trundle's goal was an absolute cracker. Although it's just a computer game, it's still difficult to score a screamer. For Trundle's goal, the ball came to us while it was in the air from 40-yards out. Jimmy, who was controlling Trundle at the time, volleyed the ball first-time, shooting the ball onto the crossbar and in. The fact that the ball hit the crossbar definitely made the goal look really spectacular. At the time it was great when we scored, as the goal put us one goal up, but soon after, it didn't make much difference to the result of the match when we found ourselves 8-3 down. We then scored two consolation goals with Jenkins (which I think was because Vernon and Ricky weren't trying as hard). Once the match had ended, Jimmy, Vernon and Ricky walked back home, as it was getting late. Katie and I then went up to our rooms to go to sleep. I needed a good night sleep, needing to fully energise myself for the trip to Renchford forest.

CHAPTER 8

Trains

Friday soon arrived, and by the time my clock had ticked to 7:40 a.m., I was out of my bed, ready to catch the train for school. Usually, my phone alarm would repeatedly go off at this time every single day. However, the alarm was surplus to requirements, as I had seemingly managed to 'programme' my body clock to wake me up at 7:40 a.m. To be honest, I find that my body clock can be really helpful, or very irritating, as it sometimes helps me get up for school in the morning, yet it can be annoying when I need some extra sleep after a late night.

This happened last year when I stayed up really late at my friend's house, as I woke up the next day at exactly 7:40 a.m., even though I was really tired. Also, this regularly occurs at the beginning of the school holidays, as it usually takes a while for my body clock to recognise that I don't have to wake up early in the morning. Annoyingly, by the time my body clock has got used to me getting up later, its then time for me to go back to school again.

At the start of the calendar year, this whole 'thing' came into play for the worse, and it was mainly because I forgot to set my alarm. It happened on the 3rd of January, my first day back at school from the Christmas holidays. Somehow, I managed to oversleep, and when I finally woke up, I remember being astonished at how light it was outside, as in January, it's usually really dark at around 7:40 a.m. (what I thought the time really was). Bemused by the cheerful daylight that was searing through the small gaps of my bedroom curtains, I escaped the enticing comfort of bed and made my way downstairs to make some breakfast. While eating a delicious bowl of organic porridge, drizzled with maple syrup, I was stunned when I glanced at my clock. It was 11:42 a.m. I had managed to oversleep after a late night of binge watching *The Inspector's Area*. I initially panicked after looking at the time, but I managed to pull myself together for a brief moment after momentarily presuming that the clock had probably lost its battery power. However, I checked my phone just to make sure and unfortunately the clock was in fact right. Whoops!

Many thoughts raced through my mind like a rollercoaster while I was thinking about how I was going to get to school for the afternoon. I then began to ponder whether to actually go to school, as I always had the option of finishing off the rest of series 2 of *The Inspector's Area*. From looking at the train times I worked out that I was projected to arrive at school halfway through the fourth lesson of the day. I wasn't sure whether it was worth the effort to go all the way to school for just 1½ lessons.

In the end, I quickly decided to book a ticket and go. It was the right decision. After logging on to the TrainSetters app, I was relieved when it I saw that there was a suitable train available for £4.57. Without hesitating, I booked a ticket, stuffed some delicious, soft, scrumptious, organic wholemeal bread into my mouth, and dashed out of my front door with my bags, ready to catch the train.

I was on my way to the train station and after looking at my watch, I was relieved when I saw that I still had 20 minutes before the train was scheduled to arrive. Unfortunately, though, it wasn't until I had been walking for 5 minutes that I realised I was still wearing my pyjama trousers. I think that I was so dopey, anxious, and desperate at the same time, that I didn't properly notice what I was actually wearing.

Before I could lose any more time, I scuppered back to the house, got changed, locked up, and then darted back towards the station as quickly as I could. This did finally put my mind to rest as to why some people were originally giving me funny looks. I then arrived at the station just as the train was about to leave. The conductor blew his whistle, and I just managed to squeeze through the doors as they were closing. The elated contentment of catching the train that I experienced was short lived, as the momentum from my jump onto the train was so great that I slammed into the closed door that was on the opposite side of the train. I must have come in pretty hard, as after I got up I noticed a small dent on the door that I crashed into. I also got a nosebleed.

I soon arrived at school 10 minutes later than I was expecting, meaning that I missed forty minutes of the history lesson before lunch, rather than the predicted thirty). I found it really awkward when I entered the classroom, as when I opened the door literally everyone began to stare at me. I was literally in the spotlight as well, as the projector light was kind of shining on me due to the projector screen being next to the door. I then tried my best to sit down in a low-key manner and let Mr Daws teach, but instead

97

he seemed to have had other ideas, as he decided to interrogate me in front of the class instead. Everyone then found out how I had overslept, how I had got a nosebleed, and how I had missed more than half of the day. To add to the already embarrassing situation, Mr Daws then slapped me with an afterschool detention. Nice.

Anyway, after momentarily contemplating the phaenomenon of body clocks, I escaped the comforts of my bed to get ready for school. In case any of you were wondering, my morning routine goes like this: wake up; eat breakfast; have a shower; get dressed; make sure I have my school stuff; brush my teeth; then leave the house (this all takes about ½ an hour). As you may have already observed, the train station is roughly a 10-minute walk away from where I live, while the train journey to school usually lasts for about 15 minutes. There's then a short 5-minute walk from the station to the school. If everything goes as planned, I get to school at about, 8:40 a.m. ready for my morning tutor group that starts at 8:45 a.m. Usually, my timings for the day run like clockwork. It's awesome.

Nevertheless, if the train happens to be late, it has a knock-on effect that results in me being late for my morning tutor group. This is particularly significant, as if someone is late for tutor group twice in the same week, they get a detention.

So, to avoid the risk of being late, my only other realistic option was to get the earlier train at 7:30 a.m. Catching this train results in me waiting around at school for an extra 45 minutes or so...which kind of sucks. My parents always seem to be worried about my usual train being late, which gets a bit annoying after a while (especially when I feel as though I have everything under control). But honestly, even if I get a few detentions from being slightly late for tutor in the morning, it's worth it considering that I am able to get an extra bit of sleep, even though I may have to miss a few lunchtimes.

As of May, I've only had two detentions from taking the later train in 3 years, so even though there was a risk of getting another detention from being late, (due to the fact that I had already been late earlier in the week) I decided to get the later train anyway. As I had a long day ahead, I reasoned that it would be important for me to get as much sleep as possible. I recognise that you may be thinking that I should simply go to bed earlier, but for some reason, I find it really hard to get to sleep if I go to bed earlier than usual. I then get worried about not getting enough sleep, which then results in me getting less sleep than usual. Currently, the only solution to this 'problem' is for me get up a lot earlier than usual so that I'm able to naturally fall asleep at an earlier time in the evening.

I constantly consider this, but I think that I'm just not willing to bear the uneasiness of getting up earlier than usual and then enduring a day of discomforting fatigue. I guess that it's another one of those life principles of sacrifice and delayed gratification. It seems that to get something meaningful, or to get what you ultimately want, you have to endure some level of discomfort and/or hardship to get it.

Although there was an undergirding threat of a detention loitering around in my mind, the real issue of being late was related to getting to school in time for the coach to Renchford Forest. It was scheduled to leave at 8:45 a.m., and I could not afford to miss it, especially as this was a huge opportunity for us to find the final clue. Here we go again.

When I arrived at the train station in the morning, a man announced on the loudspeaker that my train was going to be eight minutes late due to "unforeseen circumstances". This was annoying. Ricky and Vernon both sensibly took the earlier train (even if it did mean that they had to hang around at school for an extra while longer). When I got off the train at 8:43

a.m., it seemed that I only had two minutes to get to school in time. Usually, the walk from the train station to the school takes about five minutes, so as soon as I got off the train, I sped across the pathways relentlessly, tripping over a public bin along the way. It really hurt.

I arrived at the school, thinking that I had missed the bus, but fortunately for me I hadn't, as everyone was still waiting for a teacher who was stuck in some traffic. Everyone was told that it would be another ten minutes before she was going to arrive, so in the end I needlessly rushed. This did get me thinking that maybe teachers should get a detention, or some sort of punishment, for being late. It just doesn't seem fair that they're allowed to be late, and us pupils aren't.

While I waited amongst my fellow students, I managed to find Vernon and Ricky. Our conversation immediately turned to our focus for the day: finding the final clue. It was only at this point that we realised that we hadn't actually envisioned how we were going to break away from the main group to look for the clue. Yes, we had been a bit sloppy in devising a plan, yet we still had a 30 minute coach ride to think of something constructive.

Once the teacher arrived, we all began to board the coach. It wasn't until this moment that we realised that we hadn't planned where we were going to sit. In this instance, as we were the first to board the coach, we decided to sit at the back. As there were five seats at the back of the bus, we were hoping to sit in three of them together so that we could discuss our plans for the trip. We took our seats at the back of the coach, but about thirty seconds later some of the cool kids came up and told us to move. It seems that at our school there's an unwritten rule where the back seats are reserved for the cool kids.

While we had an awkward stand-off, Keith (one of the cool kids) took note of the map that was in my hand and ferociously attempted to snatch it from me. Fortunately, I anticipated this and quickly moved it away before he could take it. I then swiftly handed the map to Ricky, who assuredly scrunched it into his bag before anyone had the chance to examine it. We knew that we would not be able to organise anything with Keith and his mates lurking about, so without hesitation, we moved elsewhere. When we got up and let the cool kids have the seats, we found ourselves in a bit of a sticky situation, as there weren't any other spare seats paired together, meaning that we had to split up and sit separately. I got a seat next to Elise though, which wasn't too bad.

As the three of us had inadvertently been separated, we reverted to texting each other on our phones. However, Ricky had to sit out on the discussions because he didn't have a phone. Because of this, the whole situation became increasingly difficult, as Ricky was the one with the map. I then needed to figure out how I was going to get the map off Ricky without drawing too much attention to myself. So, when the teachers weren't looking, I attempted to get up and go towards Ricky's seat. Because I had a window seat, it meant that I needed to find a way past Elise without arousing suspicion. Thankfully, Elise didn't pay much attention to me when I got out of my seat. I then stealthily went towards the middle-back part of the bus, where Ricky was sitting.

Without thinking (probably because I was a bit flustered), I bluntly asked Ricky to pass the map to me. As soon as I said the word 'map', a feeling of regret immediately swallowed me up, as Paul (who was sitting next to Ricky) subsequently became interested in the object that Ricky was passing to me. I really didn't want Paul of all people to ask us about our quest, as he had a strong reputation for being unable to keep secrets. So, before he could ask me about anything, I quickly took the map off Ricky and raced back to my seat.

As I sat back down, I had difficulty in taking a proper picture of the map and sending it to Vernon, as Elise was seemingly becoming suspicious as to what I had. I was concerned that I was not going to be able to take the picture, so in a consequent moment of haste, I turned around with my back to her and quickly took a snap of the map. As I was taking the picture, Elise managed to look over and catch a glimpse of the map. It seemed that in this situation, the more that I tried to avoid Elise's attention, the more curious she became.

She then began to ask questions about the map. I tried to keep her out of the quest, as I desperately didn't want her to tell anyone else (especially Paul). The last thing I wanted was for the Year 9 Geography field trip class to turn into a school treasure hunt! Nevertheless, after eventually coming to terms with the likelihood of the day becoming increasingly difficult if I ignored her, I decided to tell her what I was up to. Ultimately I 'played' the double bluff and just told her the truth, anticipating that she would think that I was joking around. I was then hopeful that this would prevent her from catching onto what we were planning.

I told her. She then laughed. In fact, she laughed so loudly that everyone on the bus began to stare at us. For some reason, other people began to laugh as well. I honestly think that along with yawning, laughing is one of the most contagious things on planet earth. I guess that she probably thought that the treasure map stuff was a bunch of baloney. And in all honesty, I was glad if it meant that she wouldn't catch on to what Ricky, Vernon, and I were planning, even if she did think that I was a bit weird.

After the atmosphere had calmed, Elise put her headphones on and quietly began to listen to some music. Vernon and I were then free to text about the plan without any unnecessary interruptions. According to our field trip timetable, we only had three hours at the forest to execute our plan, as we were scheduled to go back to school for lunch. This was a potential blow, as we were hoping to use the lunchbreak as the opportune time to look for the last clue. After further observance of the timetable, we learnt that during one of the assigned tasks, we were scheduled to be split up in into groups of seven to do some 'quadrant sampling'.

This was to be done after an hour of strolling around doing some profiling on the forest environment. We had to observe differences in each area of the forest caused by humans, such as the amount of litter. This contributed towards a part of our reports on the trip that we would have to write at school, after lunch. Unfortunately, the three of us were all put into different groups. It seems likely that the teachers at my school deliberately split friendship groups up when they can. Maybe it's just a coincidence, but it's happened so many times with me. Although at first it felt as if this had made it more difficult for us to meet up together, in a weird way it was technically better, as if we were all in the same group, three people missing from a group of seven would be a lot more noticeable in comparison to one. We then looked ahead to the trip, readying ourselves to find the final clue.

CHAPTER 9

The Geography field trip

When we finally arrived at the forest and got off the coach, Vernon and I went over to Ricky to inform him of the plan. We had decided to meet at the oak tree, which according to the map was where the treasure was located. About one and a half hours after we had started our profiling task, I tentatively looked for a way to fade away from my group. Amidst the uncertainty of making a clean breakaway, my mind was tumbling with wisps of anxiety at the possibility of missing out on a golden opportunity to find the clue.

The clock wouldn't stop ticking, and in my mind I just envisioned Ricky and Vernon waiting for me by the tree. I think that my group could sense that something wasn't quite right with me, as apparently, I "seemed anxious" and "quiet". Fortunately, I soon found a potential getaway opportunity when my group was in deep discussion over who the designated 'measurer' was, and whether we had been sampling the correct plants. I knew that this was my chance, and so I made my move. Whoosh.

As I eased myself away from my group and moved behind some bushes, I had doubts as to whether I had managed to break away from the group without any of my peers noticing. And I also came to another hurdle, as I wasn't exactly sure where the oak tree was. I went to message Vernon, but unfortunately, I couldn't get a signal. After wandering about for five minutes, I finally saw this really big oak tree that stood out in the distance. It looked as if it was about three hundred yards away. For some reason, I just knew that this was the tree.

I managed to get to the oak tree, and when I did, I was relieved to see that Vernon was already there, but for some reason, Ricky wasn't. Vernon said that he had only just got to the tree as well, so I was glad that I took a more 'calculated' approach to sneaking away. By standing at the bottom of the tree, we were able to observe that from about 20 ft. up, there was some sort of opening in the tree. It wasn't that large, but it looked big enough for one of us to get in. We guessed that this was where the clue would be. Before we climbed up, we decided to wait for

Ricky, but after about five minutes, Vernon and I both agreed that because of the time, we should crack on with the task in hand without Ricky (we didn't exactly have bags of time). You may think that five minutes isn't long enough for us to wait for Ricky, but for some reason, time seems to go a lot more slowly when waiting.

So, we had seemingly been successful in executing the first part of our plan by getting to the tree, but we hadn't put much thought into how we were going to climb it. After a brief discussion, Vernon agreed to climb up the tree, as he had some valuable climbing experience from his time in the boy scouts. Vernon is like a squirrel when it comes to climbing trees. I reckon that he could have done some more climbing when we were in the cave as well.

I was glad that Vernon was able to climb, as I'm pretty useless when it comes to climbing trees. I certainly wish that I could climb them, and I've tried and tried, but I guess that I just wasn't made to be a climber. In the house that I used to live in when I was a lot younger (I think I was about four), there was a particular tree that I would climb up so I that could get into my next-door neighbour's back garden to play. The tree wasn't particularly high, yet I remember that I always struggled to climb it. To overcome this barrier, I would drag my climbing frame across the garden to the tree so that I could climb onto it. Annoyingly, my parents would then move the climbing frame back to its 'proper place' in the garden, meaning that when I wanted to go back into our garden from my neighbour's house, I would usually end up stuck in the tree. One time, I jumped down from the tree and badly damaged my ankle - I wasn't able to walk on it for about two weeks. Although it was a painful experience, I did appreciate getting treats and attention from everyone. After about a week though, everyone began to treat me the same again, only this time I had a badly hurt ankle. So, in this situation I was thankful that Vernon was good at climbing trees. Otherwise, I don't know what we would've done.

When Vernon got near to the hole in the tree, he became shocked at how big it was. In fact when he went inside the tree, it was so big that he was able to stand up and move around. It was like a mini-den. Although it was exciting, he experienced difficulty in finding the last clue. There were a lot of twigs and leaves which significantly contributed to the struggle in finding the last clue.

While I was keeping watch, I was met with a surprise – Elise had followed me. It seemed that she had put two and two together and realised that my disappearance from the group correlated with what I told her on the coach.

I was quite annoyed that she noticed me wander off when the rest of the group were sampling. However, she was quite upset with me for "ditching" the rest of the group, and leaving everyone else to do the group work. I then sprung up a defence that I hadn't actually ditched her and that I had already told her the reason for why when we were on the coach together. However, she wasn't convinced with my story and thought that I was simply being lazy, especially as I was on my phone when she saw me leaning against the tree. However, when Vernon came down from the tree with an envelope, I think she soon realised that we weren't messing around. I then recognised that we had to let Elise know the basics of what we were doing, just in case she went and told everyone else.

After explaining certain aspects of our quest to Elise, I suddenly wondered where Ricky had got to. My mind was put to rest on this matter, as Ricky then messaged me (using someone else's phone) to say that because he was enjoying sampling so much, he said that he would not be joining up with us. The phone signal was still pretty poor, but thankfully I found an area where I was able to pick up texts. He also said that it would be better if he didn't come, as if too many of us were at the oak tree, he said that there would probably be a higher chance of us being spotted. I think that he had a good point, and we were doing fine without him. It was just a shame for him to "miss-out" on this part of the adventure.

After I had messaged Ricky, Vernon showed Elise and I the contents of the small brown envelope that he had found. He then opened it and I was half-expecting what I saw – it was a riddle:

"I'll tell you where the treasure is hidden,

In a place where beautiful play is ridden,

People pay to go there for a short while

But not everyone usually goes home with a smile,

People sometimes go there for a break,

Possibly gulping down an invigorating milkshake,

This is a place in London, where history is made,

With it, you will be relieved of the need to be payed."

As soon as I read it, I knew that it was football themed, although, I was surprised at how cheesy the riddle was. It was as if a ten-year-old had written it as

112

a poem in a literacy class - and I'm sorry if that's offensive to people who are ten. From reading the riddle, it was also evident that the treasure was located at the Capital City Stadium in London. This is where the English Cup Final is played annually and so it was bound to be where 'history is made'. I was happy that I could finally put my football knowledge to some use. My suggestion was further supported after speaking on the phone to Butch, as he told us that from reading some information that he had found on the rich man, it turned out that he owned part of the Capital City Stadium and that he regularly attended high-profile football matches that were played there.

After it seemed that we had successfully identified where the treasure was, we somehow needed to think of how we were going to enter into the Capital City Stadium. As the Cup Final was only a day away, I thought that this would be a good opportunity to get into the stadium. However, we realised that this would virtually be impossible unless we had £200 each to buy the last few remaining tickets. Suddenly I remembered: Roger Jenkins had given Vernon, Ricky and I a free ticket each, and they weren't just any tickets – they were Exclusive, Deluxe, VIP tickets, meaning that we had access to the tunnel area. This was just what we needed!

At this point, Elise dropped the news that her dad was going to be working as a security guard for the Cup Final. This was brilliant, as she said that she would be able to find us a detailed layout of the stadium, in addition to some of her dad's security files related to the Cup Final by going onto his computer. Everything was beginning to fall into place perfectly. We then decided that it would useful for us to do some research on the stadium after school had finished, helping us to plan out an efficient method for how we were going to get the treasure. So that we could plan everything together as a group, I sent a message to everyone on the group chat, inviting them over to my house for a meeting. Elise was invited, as it turned out that she would possibly be able to help us after all.

The three of us who were at the oak tree then went back to our groups. Fortunately, mine and Elise's group didn't really notice that we had left. I mean, they knew that we had gone, but I guess that they presumed that we had gone to the toilet or something. For the rest of the trip, I found it very difficult to focus on school work, as all I was thinking about was the meeting at my house and the possibility of finding the treasure in London. I was pretty nervous, as the security at the English Cup Final is very high to say the least, so it was great that Elise was able to access some of her dad's security files.

On the coach journey back to the school, Elise and I discussed other elements of the quest. It turned out that Elise would be more important to us than I first thought, as I learnt that she also had a VIP ticket to the game, while her dad was going to be working in the tunnel area as well. The fact that she had an all access ticket like me was really helpful, as it gave her a proper opportunity to practically help us on the day.

I also did a bit of background research on the stadium while I was on my phone, just to see if I could gather any important information for the meeting. I then messaged Vernon and Ricky about spending some of our lunchtime in L6 to plan for our mission. As the computers in L6 are in high demand at lunchtimes, we recognised that we needed to get there before anyone else. Elise also said that she would join us after she had got some lunch.

Our Coach arrived back at school, and as soon as I was allowed to step off the coach, I headed straight towards L6. I set off with an attitude that nothing was going to stop me from getting to one of the computers first. In the end it turned out that I didn't need to walk in haste, as nobody else was in the room when I got to L6, apart from Mr Potts of course.

I then logged onto the computer and began doing my research.

Vernon, Ricky, and Elise soon joined me, and I was really thankful to Vernon when he let me have half of his cheeseburger. I was actually really hungry, as I had completely forgotten about having lunch. The time flew by while we were doing extensive research. We learnt a lot. However, although we managed to learn a lot, I wasn't too sure on how the information could aid us practically. We still didn't discard anything. Instead we sent everything that we thought might be helpful to us to Butch and Millie to see if any of the information would prove to be valuable to them.

After lunch had finished, I went through to tutor before I had my last lesson, which was ICT. Although I was tempted to do some research on the computers in relation to the mission, I thought better of it. It was especially important that I didn't wander onto anything associated with the quest, as my ICT teacher has this special 'spy' software installed into his classroom computers that enables him to see exactly what everyone in the class is doing.

The journey home was relatively untroubled. In fact, after what had happened the previous day (when we missed the train), we got to the train station

15 minutes earlier than usual. I found it boring to wait around, yet it was comforting to know that I wasn't going to miss the train.

As soon as I got home, I thought that it would be important for me to tell my parents that I was inviting some people around. Thankfully, they were fine with this as long as I didn't disturb them (they had a very important video conference related to their work). As Butch was in London, he had to join in on the meeting over the phone, meaning that Millie had to come over on the train (as she wasn't able to get a lift with Butch). As Elise lives about 10 minutes away, she was able to come, while Vernon and Ricky both live in the same housing estate as me, so they were both fine to come over as well.

Everyone was at my house by 7 p.m. Elise managed to bring some of her dad's files on a memory stick, while the rest of us also managed to bring other pieces of research that we had done.

Together, we had a deeper look at the history and layout of the Capital City Stadium. The stadium was built in 1900 to mark the new century, and was constructed with a network of underground tunnels. According to a history page that I found on the internet, these were later filled in for security reasons. Yet, there was a theory that went around speculating that the constructors were not able to find one of the tunnels. From this, some people believed that there was still a tunnel somewhere leading into the stadium.

Interestingly, Butch then said that when he was searching for an ancient artefact near a construction site in 2013, he stumbled across a network of underground tunnels underneath central London.

I was surprised that they had underground tunnels in London, yet apparently many had been dug to help build the parts of the London underground.

Butch then went on to say that while he had been exploring during the day, he had managed to find access to a tunnel that he had found in 2013 through an old sewage system that closed down in the 1960's, and from his extensive research into the area, he said that he was 99% sure that it was the "lost" tunnel that led to the tunnel area of the Capital City Stadium.

This seemed to fit together with the research that some of us had undertaken, as the main proponents of the theory about the "lost" tunnel believe that the tunnel can be accessed through an old sewage system that closed down in 1968. From this it seemed definite that Butch had found the tunnel.

As Millie and Butch didn't have a ticket to the game, we originally agreed that it was best if they both went through the sewers. However, as I didn't see the point of them both going (I thought that it would be easier for them to get caught), we agreed for Millie to sit this one out. She was disappointed at first, but after recognising that it was best for everyone, she fully accepted the decision.

We then had a look at the security files together, and we weren't surprised to see that the tunnel didn't show up anywhere. On the day, our plan was for Butch to message us once he had entered through the internal entrance to the tunnel. Once we found the treasure, we would then hand it down to Butch, who would then take it back through the tunnel, before getting into the getaway vehicle with Millie.

Once we had gone over everything, Vernon suggested that we should think of a special codename for the mission like they do in spy movies. Ricky thought of calling it "Operation Capital Crunch". After thinking of several different names, we struggled to think of a name that sounded better than this. Just as we were about to settle with Ricky's name for the mission, I thought of the name "Operation Golden Goal". As soon as I said it, everyone agreed that this is what we should call it. It was settled, Operation

Golden Goal was planned and ready for us to execute on the day of the Cup Final.

We went into the kitchen to have some rice cakes that had just been baked. As we all had a big day ahead of us, everyone else left shortly after we had eaten the rice cakes. When I went up to my room to get ready for bed, I was met with a pleasant reminder: my football kit had been neatly laid out. This reminded me that I was going to be playing in a football match on the following morning. This wasn't just any football match though – it was the most important match of the season. I then put my pyjamas on, brushed my teeth, and got ready to go to sleep.

CHAPTER 10

Football

6 a.m. I don't usually wake up this early on the weekends, but as I had a big day ahead of me, I was eager to get up. I was already anticipating how I was going to execute the mission, but the fact that I also had a football match of my own gave me a strong appetite for life. Having our final match of the season on the 19th May was a bit strange, as for us, the season usually finishes on the last Saturday in April. The season was finishing later than usual because of the heavy snow that my local area experienced in January and February. It actually got pretty bad at one point. Well, bad for some people, because for me it was brilliant! The heavy snowfall really helped me as on the night before it snowed, I was dreading the thought of going back to school, as I was told that we

had a week of "mid-year school assessment progress mock exams".

Apparently, we were told before Christmas, that we had these exams, while we were also expected to revise for them over the course of the Christmas holidays. Seemingly, the results of these exams were going to heavily influence the set that we would be in for our GCSE's. Somehow, I was unaware of the exams until the day before we were due to sit the first one. It was only thanks to Ricky asking me how my revision was going that I actually found out. When he first messaged me, I was a bit confused, and I just thought that he was trying to be funny. He then thought that I was the one who was messing around with him. It wasn't until he sent me a photo of his revision notes (along with a printout of the exam timetable), that I actually believed him. I then panicked a bit as my parents have really high expectations of me, which meant that I desperately needed to get some good results. I think that I probably should have checked my emails more in the run-up to the exam week, as when I logged on to my school email account that evening, I had twelve unread emails related to the exams.

Something similar also happened when I was in Year 7. The only real difference was that we were meant to be working on a project rather than preparing for an exam. As I was in middle school back then I didn't have a school email account, so the only way to know about an exam/assessment was to listen to the teacher in class. Somehow, I only learnt about the project a day before it was due in. I think it was because I was off sick on the days that the teachers talked about the project. Although there were times when I heard teachers talk to us about some sort of project, I was too shy to ask them about it, as I was scared that they would tell me off and make me look stupid in front of the class.

When it actually came to composing the project, I mostly resorted to the use of pictures to fill up some pages, in addition to making the size of the text really big (which was mainly copied and pasted from the internet, although, I did slightly alter the text to make it look like it was all my own work). I then put my work in a folder to make it look like I had put in more effort than I actually had. I was super-excited after I had done twelve pages of "work". Yet, some doubts crept into my mind on the following morning, as I wasn't sure whether my last-ditch efforts would be good enough, seeing as the teachers were expecting six weeks of work on the topic of spies. In the end, I got a level 5b grade for my work. For one night's work, this was pretty decent.

Anyway...because of the snowy weather throughout January, many of my games were postponed, meaning that they had to be rescheduled. As the final match of the season was due to kick off at 10:30 a.m., it meant that I had plenty of time to get to the Capital City Stadium for the Cup Final (kick-off for this was 5:30 p.m.). I didn't get much sleep in the night. I think that it was because on the night before I have a match, I usually contemplate how I'm going to score and the way in which I'll celebrate and stuff like that. But it's annoying, as due to all of the excitement, it means that I can't get enough sleep and then when the match arrives, I'm sometimes not able to play to my full potential due to being sleep deprived.

Although I was excited when I got out of bed, the night's sleep was a lot tougher than usual, as I was thinking about the quest. I do find sleep to be a very ambivalent concept, in that when I have a hard day ahead, I feel more tired than I usually would. And then on Saturday mornings, I get excited because I know that I don't have school in the morning, resulting in me getting up out of bed a lot earlier than usual. It's really annoying. I just wish that it was the other way around, as I would then find it easy to get up early for school, while I would also be able to experience a nice Saturday morning lie-in.

As I still had a football match to play, I followed my natural matchday routine. As soon as I got out of my bed, I changed into my football kit. For Kettleston Rovers, I wear the number 11 shirt, the same shirt number as Charlie Trundle for Westminster Warriors. I'm bittersweet towards wearing this shirt number, as I appreciate wearing a number that is from 1-11 (it half-shows that I'm usually in the starting line-up). However, after my outstanding season last year as the club's top goalscorer with 18 goals, I was expecting to be given the then-vacant No. 10 shirt, as I was going to be allocated a new number for the new season (I previously had the No. 33 shirt). To my disappointment, the coach's son, Callum, was given the No. 10 shirt instead. After a while, it didn't really bother me much, it's just that because of the shirt number font, it looks like I have a pause button symbol plastered on the back of my shirt whenever I wear it.

Once I had my full kit on, I went downstairs to make myself some breakfast. On school days I normally go for some wheat biscuits, as they are quick and easy to make, but as I had more time for preparation, I decided to cook myself a full English breakfast. It was very tasty. I highly recommend adding a splash of Worcester Sauce – it takes the dish to another level.

After I had finished my breakfast, I still had a couple of hours to spare before I needed to leave for my pre-match warm-up. As everyone else in the house was still in bed, I had an opportune time to play some football on the MegaWay 5 undisturbed. My favourite mode on the MegaWay 5 is internet leagues. I'm currently in a league with 11 other people from my school. When I logged on to play I was in 5th place, yet I was also only 8 points off the top of the league with about 6 matches to play. I was still able to mathematically win. This was unlikely though, as Gary (who was at the top of the league) had been on a 7-game winning streak. As it was still very early, I wasn't very optimistic about finding someone else from the league to play. However, after sending out a message on the group chat, Gary and Elliott both said that they were available to give me a game. I played Elliott first. As he was ranked last in the league with 1 point, I saw this as an opportunity for me to warmup for the game against Gary.

So, I played Elliott and won 2-0. The game was actually a lot more difficult than I first expected, with Elliott having a lot of chances in the first half. He nearly took the lead with a 30 yard strike that cannoned of the bar and onto the goal line. I got a bit nervous at halftime with the scores level at 0-0, so changed to an attacking formation of 4-2-1-3. The change of formation made all the difference, with Charlies Trundle scoring 2 quick-fire goals at the start of the second half. Boom.

I decided to stick to this formation for the game against Gary. It worked really well for me during the first half, with my team going in at half-time 3-0 up. I don't think that Gary was expecting me to go out and brutally attack him the way I did. He did a bit of tweaking to his team at half time and managed to expose some gaps in my defence to make it 3-1 straight away. As I then had a 2-goal advantage, I decided to 'shut up shop' and 'park the bus'. My formation changed from 4-2-1-3, to 5-3-2. As crazy as it sounds, I even put Roger Jenkins in defence, as I knew that he was good at winning headers. For the remainder of the second half, Gary's team came at me with a very attacking style of play. On many different occasions, it looked as if he was going to score, especially when he somehow managed to miss an open goal from 8 yards out. In the end I held onto my lead, winning the match by 2 goals. After winning, I was only 2 points off Gary at the top of the league (however, he still had a game-in-hand).

It was then time to play some real football. I soon arrived at the Kettleston playing fields. We had a warm-up where we jogged around our half of the pitch, doing stretches at each corner flag and at each side of the half-way line. We did some basic 1-to-1 passing drills, before finally moving onto the shooting drills. After this, we had a team talk with our coach. It was then nearly time for kick-off.

We were playing against Harlsbury Swifts. They were our nearest competitors in our division, with both of us battling against each other to avoid relegation. In our league, only one team gets relegated. We were in Division 3 of our local league and we didn't really fancy dropping down to Division 4 (the bottom league for our age-group). Before we kicked-off we occupied the bottom space, but because we were 1 point below our opponents, we needed a win to avoid getting relegated, while Harlsbury only needed to draw.

For the team talk, our manager mainly told us to "keep it tight in midfield", and "play it on the floor". Most of the stuff that our manager says doesn't usually make much sense to me. I mean, if you "play it on the floor", how are you supposed to score headers? Surely all you have to do is get the ball through the goal posts. How hard can it be? Well, obviously very hard for us, as we were bottom of the league. We were playing a 4-3-3 formation. My preferred position is striker, but for this match I was forced out wide on the right to make way for Callum, who was chosen to play on his own up-front. Out of the three forward positions, I find that playing on the right is the most difficult because it means that I'm not able to cut in onto my stronger foot to have a shot – although, I can still whip some balls into the box.

The game kicked off, and it was quite scrappy to begin with, as most of the play in the early stages took place in midfield, with tackles flying in from all over the place. Very few chances opened up from this sticky period of play. However, after 11 minutes we managed to threaten the opposition goal when our goalkeeper, Nick, kicked the ball further than usual from a goal kick. A defender who was marking me went up for a header, but missed the ball by jumping too early. I anticipated this and managed to run onto the loose ball. If I was more central, I would have been through on goal, but as I was on the wing the most effective way for me to attack was to dribble down the right-hand side of the pitch.

I sprinted down the right wing with the ball, and then as I got near to the corner flag, whipped the ball into the box, hoping that someone would be on the receiving end of it for a tap-in. As I crossed the ball in, Callum made a brilliant run into the box, darting past several defenders. He ran towards the front post as the ball raced towards him. Suddenly, Callum lost his balance and somehow managed to hit the cross bar from 5 yards out, the ball rebounded onto the goalkeeper's face, causing the ball to deflect onto both posts. Their best defender slid in to hook the ball off the line. No goal!

This was honestly one of the worse misses that I had witnessed during a football match. If I was the manager, I would have changed the striker immediately. There were not any other clear-cut chances until the 40th, which is when Harlsbury were awarded their first corner of the match. This all came about from one of our defenders doing an awful pass back to the goalkeeper. It was about to be an own goal, but our goalkeeper did an amazing save by diving full stretch to keep the ball out for a corner kick. From the following corner, the Harlsbury corner-kick-taker whipped in a decent cross towards the back post. One of their defenders then jumped up and headed the ball onto the crossbar and in. I felt that we were a bit hard done by, and that we had definitely deserved to be in the lead.

We finished the first half trailing 1-0. I was expecting our manager to be really disappointed, while I was also concerned that I would be substituted off, yet he was actually really positive and optimistic. I felt that this gave our team an emotional and mental lift. In the end, he only made one substitution. He substituted Kyle, our defensive midfielder, for Lawrence, who usually played as an attacking midfield player. The manager then told us to "pretend that the score is 0-0, and keep doing what you're doing". This didn't make much sense to me, as if we continued to play the way that we had, we would lose the match 2-0.

From the first 5 minutes of the second half, substituting Lawrence on for Kyle seemed like a tactical masterstroke from our manager, as Lawrence completely changed the dynamic of the match in our favour. We were more fluid in our attacks, meaning that we were able to put the opposition team on the back foot. I think that another reason why Harlsbury were playing more defensively was because they only needed a draw from the match to avoid relegation, meaning that they had a 1 goal safety net at this point of the match.

After about 57 minutes, Lawrence played a one-two with Callum in the box before readying himself for a shot. As Lawrence was about to shoot, a Harlsbury defender slid in to try and stop the shot, consequently hacking Lawrence to the ground. The referee immediately pointed to the penalty mark. Penalty! This was a lifeline, and a great opportunity for us to level the scores at 1-1. I was desperate to have this. Taking a penalty is like a free shot. I went straight to the ball and grabbed it. Callum then tried to take the ball off me, resulting in a bit of a spat between the two of us. To resolve the issue, the manager shouted from the touchline that I could take it. I placed the ball on the penalty mark while feeling incredibly nervous. My legs were like jelly, but I tried not to show it. I decided to aim for the left-hand side of the goal, as I went this way when I scored my previous penalty. I stepped up to take the penalty and side-footed the ball towards the left corner of the goal. The goalkeeper correctly guessed where I was going, sensationally making a one-handed save to deny me. I was gutted. I had let everyone down.

I trudged around for the next 30 minutes, thinking about how much I had let my teammates down. The penalty miss definitely affected my personal performance in a negative way, as I was constantly worried that I was on the verge of being substituted. The substitution never came. During the last parts of the game, we managed to conjure up several good chances, but unfortunately, we failed to score from any of them. Our team dominated the second half, and it felt like there was some sort of force field around the opposition goal.

All of a sudden, we found ourselves playing into stoppage time at the end of the match. I thought that we were heading for a defeat. We then had a corner which Lawrence took by curling the ball into the box. As expected, one of their defenders easily headed the ball out of the box. As I was standing on the edge of the box, the ball that had been headed out looped up in front of me. I was really tired at this point and so I decided to kick the ball as hard as I could back towards the goal. I managed to make a good connection with the ball. The ball was travelling directly towards the goalkeeper, who was getting ready to catch it. However, before the ball could get to him, it hit of one of the Harlsbury defenders, causing the ball to deflect into the corner of the goal. The goalkeeper was completely wrong-footed, standing helplessly as the ball flew past him.

I couldn't believe it – I had just scored. This was my 11th goal of the season. At this point we all started to believe that we could score a winning goal and pull off an extraordinary comeback. I picked the ball up out of the net and ran back to the centre circle to save as much time as I could (and also to maintain our newly found momentum). I asked the referee how long we had left to play. He said 30 seconds.

As soon as the Harlsbury players restarted the game with a kick-off, our team charged towards them, hoping to get the ball as soon as we could. Our left winger, Sam, did a crunching tackle on their striker, winning the ball fairly. He then passed the ball to me on the right-hand side of the pitch. I then controlled the ball, and chipped the ball over to Lawrence who was in the centre of the pitch. Lawrence then dribbled past 3 Harlsbury players, before sliding the ball through to Callum, who had made a brilliant run on the left wing.

Callum skilfully controlled the ball, before cutting in onto his right foot and whipping the ball into the box. They then headed the ball away. I anticipated where the ball would go, and just like my first goal, I was positioned perfectly to strike an oncoming ball from the edge of the box. This was the moment that I had been waiting for. As my foot came into contact with the ball, the connection felt perfect. It was like poetry in motion. I was certain that I was going to score. In fact, I think that the contact with the ball was probably sweeter than it was for my first goal.

The ball then soared towards the top corner of the goal. I was getting ready to wheel away in celebration. Somehow, the Harlsbury goalkeeper managed to fingertip the ball into the post. The ball rebounded off the post, and into the path of Sam, who then blazed the ball over the bar from 10 yards. It was virtually an open goal, as the keeper was on the floor from when he dived to save my shot. The referee then blew his whistle to signal the end of the game. The match finished 1-1, meaning that we had been relegated to Division 4. I was very disappointed, but after missing the chances that we had, we probably didn't deserve to be in Division 3 anyway.

The rest of the team were also very disappointed. Nick was even in tears shortly after the game as well. Our manager then gave us a team talk at the end congratulating us on our "valiant" efforts, before saying that we should all "be proud of ourselves". This certainly improved the mood within the team.

After an uplifting post-match team talk from the manager, my mood began to drop down again, as I found myself waiting in the car park for one of my parents to pick me up. After waiting for 15 minutes, I decided to start walking towards my house, as I thought that this would make the time go by more quickly, while it would also make the journey shorter for my mum or dad. After walking for ten minutes, other parents from the players of my team began to drive back and offer me a lift. I didn't want to trouble any of them, and I thought that it was cooler to be independent, so I politely declined. It wasn't until the manager pulled up and strongly encouraged me to get a lift home that I finally gave in.

His car had been fitted with some plush leather seats, making the ride a very comfortable experience. However, after a couple of minutes had passed, I awkwardly noticed my mum drive straight past us. I wasn't even sure if my manager had noticed that it was my mum who had just driven by. While I was in the car, I quickly texted my mum to let her know that I was getting a lift. My mum was really annoyed with me when she came back home, and told me to always wait at the playing fields if she was ever late again.

I then went upstairs and had a refreshing cold bath. While I was cooling down, I briefly reflected on the disappointment of being relegated, but after logically thinking about the concept of relegation, I was actually quite excited to play in Division 4, as the teams would probably be easier to play against. I was also hopeful of having more opportunities to score goals.

After feeling refreshed from my bath, I went downstairs to make myself a ham and cheese sandwich. It was delicious! While I was consuming the last part of the sandwich, I looked at the clock. It was 2 p.m.! This meant that I only had ten minutes to get to the train station in time. It looked like there was going to be another race against the clock!

CHAPTER 11

The Capital City Stadium

I managed to get onto the train with only a few seconds to spare before the doors closed. Although it was close, it was nowhere near as theatrical as the other day when I missed it (it was still dramatic though). After boarding the train, I quickly found Ricky and Vernon. They had saved me a seat next to them with a table, which was ideal as it meant that it was easier for us to talk to each other.

We managed to fully consolidate our plan within the first thirty minutes of our train journey. This was the final plan: after getting through to our VIP seats, we would roam around in the tunnel area using our VIP passes (kindly given to us by Roger Jenkins); the three of us would go to the toilets that were near the dressing rooms and change into a Westminster

Warriors football kit with a bib on, creating the illusion that we were reserve substitutes; Butch would then hopefully come up from an opening in the floor dressed as a security guard. To be honest, I still did not know too much about this "secret tunnel" and how Butch was planning to get into the stadium toilets through it. When I tried to get more information about it from him, he just said to trust him and that he had "everything under control". Just in case Butch went missing, we had a Plan B.

Once Butch had properly entered the stadium, the plan was for him to imitate a security guard by standing next to the door outside of the dressing rooms, acting as if he was meant to be there. In case he was asked for his security badge, Vernon managed to make him a fake one based on a picture of the one that Elise's dad had - we weren't sure whether this would work though. To some degree, this was one of the riskiest parts of our plan. To avoid arousing suspicion, we hoped to avert the attention of the actual security guard who was meant to be there thanks to Elise. Elise didn't say how she would do this, but we trusted her, especially as the actual security guard who was meant to be on duty was in fact her dad.

The three of us would then get the treasure, put it in a football kit bag to avoid suspicion, hand the bag to Butch, who would then go to the tunnel opening (wherever it was) and escape. While Butch escaped, the rest of us would watch the rest of the English Cup Final (it would be a shame to waste a VIP ticket). This was just the basic plan. Obviously there was a chance that it wouldn't go as smoothly as we planned, yet we knew that we had to be hopeful and positive for us to have the best chance of things working out.

After we went through the plan, we sat through the rest of the journey talking about our pre-match predictions for the Cup Final. It was a bit awkward how I supported Westminster, as Ricky and Vernon both supported Hibblesbury. Whenever something like this came up, I was always subtly accused of being a glory supporter. In my defence though, Westminster were the first team that I saw play at a stadium live, while the first football shirt that I ever owned was a Westminster Warriors one. To make things a bit more awkward for me, the train was packed full of Hibblesbury supporters while I was wearing my Westminster Warriors shirt with pride. We soon arrived at the nearest station to the stadium (which was virtually two minutes away from the stadium).

By the time we got to our VIP seats, kick-off was only ten minutes away. Being very close to the tunnel, our seats were in the perfect location for our quest. Our VIP tickets also enabled us to roam around the tunnel area up to five minutes before kick-off. Very soon, the players were going to be walking out, ready for the national anthem to be sung. I was eager to proceed ahead with the plan, but as part of it I still needed to wait for a text from Butch to say that the coast was clear (Butch was also waiting for a message from Elise). We had our kits in our bags ready, and as the clock precariously ticked closer towards the kick-off time, we decided that the right thing to do was for us to head over to the tunnel area regardless. Quickly, we confidently walked through the tunnel area. Thankfully, we weren't approached by anyone asking for ID or anything like that.

However, Roger Jenkins approached us and asked us how we were all doing. He said that he remembered us from my social media during the week. It was a bit awkward when he offered to sign the jumper that he gave me from school, as I forgot all about it. This was mainly because I had directed so much of my focus towards finding the treasure. Nevertheless, he was cool about the situation and said that it didn't really matter. He then went back into the home dressing room and went to get each of us a signed football so that we at least had something with his autograph on.

After he came back with the signed footballs, I was also able to get a cheeky selfie with him. Once all of the other players began to come out of the dressing rooms, I saw this as my cue to leave. We then walked towards the toilets to change into our football kits, and hopefully, meet with Butch. Fortunately, I had been able to go on a stadium tour of the Capital City Stadium as part of a school trip when I was in Year 7, meaning that I was able to remember where the toilets were.

Once we were in the toilets, we waited there for a message from Butch that would give us the go-ahead for when we should enter the home dressing room (as this is where we thought the treasure was). We were discussing the final run-through of our plan, but we suddenly had to stop talking when someone came into the toilets. It was Benny Kerson, the Hibblesbury manager. To avoid any sort of suspicion, the three of us had to stop what we were doing and pretend that we were using the facilities.

I think that he was slightly bemused as to what was really happening, especially as Vernon decided to wash his hands before going to the toilet. As he left, I could tell that he was nervous. I wasn't sure whether it was because of the situation or the fact that his team were about to play Westminster Warriors. Either way, I kind of felt sorry for the guy.

Shortly after Kerson had left, I began to hear a clambering racket from beneath my feet. The floor then began to viciously vibrate. I went outside the cubicle that I was in to observe my surroundings. I was a bit concerned about our plan going to shreds, as if someone came in it was likely that our cover would be blown. I then flushed all of the toilets and turned on the taps in an attempt to drown out the noise. Thankfully, the noise didn't go on for much longer. The noise slowly began to quieten down and some of the tiles on the flooring began to break open, forming a small hole, big enough for a human to squeeze through. All of a sudden, Butch came up out of the floor!

Funnily enough, this secret underground tunnel led to…the toilets! This was handy, as we didn't need to wait for a text message from Butch (although, he still needed to wait for a message from Elise). I didn't know how Elise was going to avert her dad's attention away from being a security guard, but she said that she had an idea of what she was going to do. Butch's phone then vibrated. He had received a message from Elise: the coast was clear. Butch, dressed in a smart black suit (that was slightly smudged), donned with black sunglasses, assuredly went out to "guard" the unguarded dressing room door. Thirty seconds later, the three of us went out of the toilets towards the dressing rooms wearing our full kits, looking like professional footballers. No one in the tunnel area batted an eyelid towards us as we managed to sneak into the home dressing room.

After Butch let us into the home dressing room, I was gobsmacked - I was actually in the Westminster dressing room for the English Cup Final! Wow! To make the most of the moment, I quickly got my phone and started to vlog the experience. The thing that amazed me the most was being able to look at the tactics board, and see how much detail there actually was. While this was happening, Vernon and Ricky were focusing on finding the final clue. Once I realised that I was wasting precious time, I swiftly joined them in the search for the treasure.

To reassure ourselves of what we were actually looking for, and where the treasure specifically was, we decided to have another look at the final clue. I mean, the dressing room was pretty big, and the fact (or presumption) that nobody else was aware of the treasure made us realise that this wasn't going to be an easy find. I then went to get the clue out of my sock. The reason it was there was because I didn't have any pockets and I didn't want to risk losing it.

It was difficult to recover the clue from my sock, as the piece of paper (that had the clue on) had somehow sunk down to where my toes were. This meant that I had to get my sock off in the dressing room. While I was getting my sock off, I momentarily experienced a glimpse of what it felt like to be a Westminster Warriors footballer who was getting ready to play in a big match. To make the most of the opportunity, I asked Vernon to take a snap of me taking my sock off, as I was fully dressed in a Westminster Warriors kit. This was the stuff of dreams. I did think about posting the photo online, but thought better of it, as the police would probably arrest me. After posing for the photo, I managed to get my hands on the piece of paper that was in my sock. My feet are prone to getting really sweaty, and so the state of the piece of paper that was in my sock was really disgusting. We even ended up using one of the hairdryers to dry it off. There was then difficulty in actually reading what it said.

Fortunately, Vernon had a picture of the clue on his phone from the day that we found it. To be honest, we probably should have just used Vernon's phone in the first place. It would have saved time. Speaking of time, Ricky then reminded us that we were still racing against the clock. Time management is definitely something that I need to work on, as throughout the day it hadn't been great. In the circumstance in which we found ourselves, the amount of time that we had depended on how long Elise could distract her dad for. Elise didn't say how long we would have specifically, so to be on the safe side we gave ourselves five minutes (it was probably better to be safe than sorry in this case).

From my interpretation that the riddle in the clue said something about the dressing room and the number ten, it seemed likely that there was a possible connection between them in relation to the specific location of the treasure within the dressing room. In regards to there being a probable connection between the dressing rooms and the number ten, it immediately seemed obvious to us that the treasure was located near the No. 10 seat inside the dressing room. When I saw who the No. 10 seat was being used by for the Cup Final, I was amazed – the clue actually led us to Roger Jenkins' seat!

As the stadium was really old, the whole set-out and architecture of the dressing room was far from modern – at first, it felt like we had gone back in a time machine. Apparently, the reason why some parts of the stadium (such as the dressing rooms) haven't been "modernised" is because the owners want to keep some parts of its historical nature.

Vernon then reached into his bag and took out a mini metal detector, before scanning the area around the No. 10 seat. I'm not sure how Vernon managed to get that thing through security, but the main thing was that he did. In fact, I had even forgotten that he had brought it with him. We heard a lot of beeps when Vernon put the detector up close to the wall behind the No. 10 seat. Although we assumed that the treasure was in the wall behind the seat, it wasn't necessarily obvious to us. After tapping the wall for a bit, it seemed to be very thin and hollow. From this it seemed likely that the treasure was hidden behind the wall. I then received a text message from Elise saying that we only had about one minute until her dad was going to come back and check the dressing rooms.

I didn't want to have gone through the difficulty that we had endured for nothing. We had gone too far too turn back. We soon discovered that the wall was in fact a big piece of chipboard that had been decorated. The three of us then managed to pull this away from the wall, revealing to us an old cardboard box. We weren't 100% sure whether this was the treasure, as the box was tightly sealed.

From looking at the time, it seemed that we only had ten seconds before Elise's dad was going to enter the room. Without a moment to lose, we carefully placed the box into a training bag that we had brought with us. The three of us then swiftly headed towards the door. As we were about to leave the dressing room, the Westminster assistant manager suddenly came in to get a notebook. When I first saw who the assistant manage was, I froze. It was Jeffrey Langston, a Westminster Warriors legend from the 1960's.

Langston had written his name into the history books as the first goalkeeper to score a hat-trick for Westminster Warriors. In fact, I think that he is also the only professional player ever to do so in England (so far). I thought that my Grandad was joking when he first told me about Langston scoring a hat-trick, but after doing some research on the internet, I was very surprised when I found out that it actually happened. After scoring 2 penalties during the game, he completed his unexpected hat-trick in the last minute of a thrilling 3-3 draw. He was on the edge of the box when a corner kick was being taken, and as a defender headed the ball out to him, he smashed the ball into the top corner of the goal. After the ball went in, there was a massive pitch invasion.

The pitch invasion was so big that the referee had to end the game slightly early because the stewards were unable to get all of the people off the pitch. After the game, some members of the media nicknamed him "long-shot Langston". This soon caught on, as most football fans then started to call him "long-shot" for short. After a while, a lot of people then started to think that this was his actual name. I actually found this quite amusing when I was reading up on him, because when Westminster players began to wear names on the back of their shirts, Langston actually got the name "long-shot" printed onto his shirt. At first the league officials didn't approve, but because of an uproar and backlash received from many football fans, they overturned the decision. This then led to other footballers getting nicknames printed onto their shirt. Things soon got a bit silly and out of hand. This was especially the case when a player called Nigel Eggleston got the name "scrambled egg" printed on his.

Anyway, after Langston walked past us to get his notebook, many thoughts raced through my mind. Part of me wanted to talk to him about his famous hat-trick, while the other part of me was worried that our cover would be blown.

Out of the blue, Langston then called the three of us over to him, using a stern tone of voice. We thought that this was it. As I turned towards him, I nearly asked him to not turn us over to the police, but before I had a chance to say anything, he asked us why we were weren't out in the dugouts. It didn't take me long to realise that Langston probably thought that we were actual players. I struggled to think of a proper excuse. I began to feel under pressure, as I realised that Langston would get suspicious of us if we didn't come up with an adequate excuse. Vernon then acted quickly by telling Langston that we were still in the dressing room because we were thirsty. After Vernon said this, I thought that our covers were going to be blown.

Unexpectedly, Langston told us to go to the dugouts as quickly as possible. To my surprise, Langston actually found Vernon's excuse to be convincing. I guess Langston thought that it would absurd to think that three random teenagers could sneak into the dressing room on the day of the English Cup Final. I think he merely presumed that we were youth players who were put into the squad for the match, so that we could experience what it is like on a match day in a major Cup Final. The three of us then left the dressing room as quickly as we could.

As the three of us left the dressing room, I went to give the bag to the person who was by the door (as I thought it was Butch). As soon as I realised that it was Elise's dad, I quickly pulled the bag away at the last second. I didn't think that he was going to be there, as I thought that he would have first walked into the dressing room to check it.

While Ricky proceeded towards the dugouts, Vernon and I went to the toilets to hand the bag to Butch. After going into the toilets, we recognised that we needed to be quiet, as both of the cubicles were in use. It then came to my attention that Butch was probably in one of them. After calling out to Butch, we were soon able to figure out which cubicle he was in. I then quietly handed the bag to Butch without saying anything, as we didn't know who was in the other cubicle. To help disguise the noises that Butch would make while he opened up the entrance to the tunnel, I turned on the taps and hand dryer, and also flushed the toilet, creating a very loud noise. Oh, and I also made some coughing noises as well.

I then went into one of the cubicles to change back into my normal clothes, as I planned on enjoying the rest of the game from my VIP seat. Mission accomplished. Well, I thought that it was until I saw another man in the cubicle. Whoops, this was awkward. For some reason I had forgotten that there was someone else in there. It was probably because I had my mind so focused on something else. I mean, it doesn't help when there's a green colour on the outside, because he forgot to lock the door. I sometimes get confused whether green means vacant or occupied (it's different in some places that I have been to).

He wasn't on the toilet though. Instead he was planting a bomb. We were both in shock at the presence of each other. I saw that there was some sort of remote in the guy's pocket and suspected that this was needed to trigger the bomb. So, in a moment of panic, and without thinking through all of the consequences of my actions, I grabbed the remote and ran. The guy then began to chase after me. Vernon was inside the other cubicle (the one that Butch was in before) getting changed when he heard me say something about a bomb.

Once the terrorist had chased me out of the toilets, Vernon went into the toilet cubicle that I was in to try and disable the bomb. It was very important he was successful in this, because if I accidentally pressed the big red button on the remote it would send the whole stadium up in flames. There weren't many places for me to run, and so I followed my natural instincts and ran down the tunnel and onto the pitch. When doing so, Vernon gave me a text message to say that the bomb had been disarmed. This was comforting news until I looked behind me and saw that the terrorist was getting closer to me. Although it might have seemed crazy to run onto the pitch, it worked in my favour to some extent, as some of the match stewards began to chase after the terrorist when we entered the pitch.

Coincidently, when I ran onto the pitch, Westminster had just won a penalty. Charlie Trundle was readying himself to the take the penalty kick. With the ball sitting on the spot, I saw a good opportunity to score a goal in a Cup Final in front of 100,000 people (yes, I knew that the goal wouldn't count, but if I don't make it as a pro footballer, this was surely the closest experience I'll ever get to it). It was also really cool that I was fully dressed in my Westminster Warriors kit (which had my name and number on the back), as I didn't have enough time to get changed back into my normal clothes. With my phone in one hand and the remote in the other (and also a terrorist chasing after me), I sprinted towards the penalty mark as fast as my legs would allow me to.

Some of the stewards then managed to tackle the terrorist, and pin him to the ground. After he had been caught, all of the stewards and security guards had turned their attention towards me. I was the sole target. As I approached the penalty area, I began to tire. Suddenly, Elise's dad came up from behind, attempting to rugby tackle me to the ground. Out of pure instinct I anticipated this, and swayed to the side to dodge the attempted takedown. Elise's dad then ended up tackling one of his colleagues to the ground instead.

As a result, some of the other security guards tripped over the two security guards who were on the ground. Because many of the stewards/security guards had fallen to the ground, a clear path to the ball opened up for me. I think that the players clearly noticed the chaos that had emerged, as they all decided to get out of the way. This was probably to avoid getting an embarrassing injury in a bizarre way. I think that the goalkeeper could sense that I was going to be taking a penalty, as he stayed on his goal line, ready for an oncoming strike.

I kicked the ball as hard as I could, aiming for the top left corner of the goal. I remembered to keep my head over the ball, preventing me from humiliating myself by kicking the ball into row Z. Instead, the ball rocketed into the top corner, past the out-stretched arm of the goalkeeper. In celebratory fashion, I ran towards the crowd and took my shirt off, before doing one of the biggest knee slides ever. I slid from the edge of the box to the touchline of the pitch. Because I carried so much momentum on the slide, I nearly slammed into the advertising hoardings. A steward tried to catch me, but the momentum from the slide sent him flying. I think that this moment of contact with the steward helped prevent me from the hitting the advertising hoardings (he slowed me down).

I got carried away with the celebrations from the crowd. Too carried away in fact, as I forgot all about the security guards, and just when I realised that they were still after me, one of them aggressively pinned me to the ground and handcuffed me. Ouch. It actually really hurt. It was the first time someone had put real handcuffs on me. They were really uncomfortable as well. I don't recommend trying them on as you will probably hurt your wrists if you lock them too tightly (this probably depends on how long you have them on for). Mine were fastened very tightly, and I had to wear them for a long time as well.

Large parts of the crowd cheered me while I was escorted past the main stand. It was a small consolation from being handcuffed. I then realised that the actual penalty was on the verge of being taken. I turned around just in time to see Charlie Trundle caress the ball into the bottom right-hand corner of the goal to level the scores at 1-1. It was a very calm finish for such an important penalty.

I was nearing the tunnel, and as I was led towards it, I looked towards the Westminster dugout to see if Ricky and Vernon were sitting there. After seeing that they were not there, I was concerned that they had also been caught. However, I found out later that Ricky and Vernon both got changed and went back to their VIP seats while I was on the pitch, as the thrill of the situation helped them, as everyone was focusing on the bizarre happenings that had unfolded on the pitch.

CHAPTER 12

Homecoming

After being escorted out of the stadium, the security guards handed me over to a group of police officers near the back entrance of the stadium. I was then hurled into the back of a police car. I was relieved when I found out that the terrorist was in a different vehicle to me (who knows what the dude would have done to me if we were in the same car together). Because of the London traffic, it took a while before we eventually arrived at the nearest Police Station. It was 8 p.m. by the time we arrived. Throughout the journey, I was desperate to know the score for the Cup Final to see if Westminster had won, yet I wasn't able to because my phone had been confiscated. From observing the reactions of some Westminster fans in several pubs that we drove past, it seemed evident that Westminster had scored after I left the stadium.

Nevertheless, I still wanted to know what the score was. I even asked the police officer who was driving the car to turn the radio on. He refused.

After slowly making our way through the heavy traffic, we finally arrived at a Police Station. Upon being pulled out of the car, I felt a shiver down my spine as I began to comprehend the gravity of the situation that I was in.

The grey, wet and cloudy weather reflected my mood as I was led into the Police Station. After I was dragged into the station, I had to wait in a cell for about thirty minutes. A police officer then came in and brought me to an office. I was given load of forms to fill in, before being questioned inquisitively by a police detective. I was then dumped back into the cell that I had been in when I first arrived at the station. I fell asleep within two minutes of entering the cell again, as the whole procedure that I had undergone had lasted about four hours.

Fourteen hours later, I woke up and found myself lying down in a completely different room, on my bed. I was in my bedroom. I was confused and seriously questioned whether or not I had dreamt about falling asleep in a Police Station – I wasn't sure whether everything that took place on the day of the Cup Final had actually happened. I looked around the house to see if anyone was around, and after looking in every room I soon found out that everyone else had gone out. I was also incredibly hungry, so I went into the kitchen to get something to eat. After sitting down to munch on a bowl of cereal, I spotted a note on the table from my mum. It basically said that everyone else had gone to church, and that they would be back after a "meeting" at the Police Station.

This made it clear to me that I wasn't dreaming. Although I was somewhat pleased that I knew where everyone was, I felt a level of uneasiness in regards to the happenings of the meeting at the Police Station. The reality of the situation was further apparent to me after I briefly skimmed through the Sunday newspaper. There were news reports related to the Cup Final everywhere! People seemed to be more interested in the terrorist plot than the actual match (which finished 2-1 to Westminster Warriors, with Roger Jenkins scoring a last-minute winner).

After finishing my breakfast, I went outside into the garden to read a book in the hope that it would help me take my mind off the news surrounding the English Cup Final. I do recommend reading a good book though (if you can ever find one). It really helps me to stretch my mind, while my parents always seem to be happy when they see me reading – in this case, it's a win-win situation.

I read my book for half-an-hour before my family then came back home. After asking them about the situation with the police, they said that everything was going to be okay and that I should rest for the remainder of the day. Ten minutes later, the police arrived at my house. I was really confused. My parents had told me that everything was going to be okay, yet the fact that the police had arrived at my house seemed to suggest otherwise. My instinctive reaction was to run away, but when I thought about this it didn't make any sense, as I had nowhere to go. Even if there was somewhere for me to run to, the police would probably find me eventually.

I was right to stay put, as it turned out that after hours of uncertainty (and after the police had examined several pieces of evidence), the police saw that I was telling the truth when I told them that I invaded the pitch to help stop the terrorist. They then apologised to me for any trouble that they had caused. To make things better, the senior officer rewarded me with £50,000 because I had helped the government (without realising it) take down the man who was No. 5 on Britain's most wanted list. One of the police officers then went on to say that he had made his way into the stadium through an underground tunnel. After asking the officer about the tunnel, it turned out that it was the same one that

Butch used! This made me very suspicious about Butch, as I seriously wondered whether he had any connections with the terrorist.

After the police and secret service discovered the existence of the tunnel, a huge investigation related to the incident was summoned. Many other tunnels around London that led to other major landmarks were also discovered. The police were shocked that this was the only plotted terrorist attack in the stadium's history. I was exhausted from all of this, and so I decided to attend an evening church service, as I live close to the church in my neighbourhood (I seriously needed a break from everything that was on the news). It was also exhausting for me when I logged into my social media, as I got thousands of notifications from random people following me.

It was a very unique experience at school on the following day, with everyone coming up to me asking about what had happened. I felt like a celebrity. At the end of the day, Vernon, Ricky, Elise, and I went into town to get a pizza. We asked Butch and Millie if they wanted to meet up with us, but they both said that they were busy with something.

While we were waiting for our pizza in the restaurant, the conversation between the four of us became interesting when our primary point of discussion turned towards the treasure quest. We began to wonder what had happened to the box that we had found, and also questioned why the four of us hadn't received our fair share. In an attempt to quench any doubt that existed between the four of us in regards to the treasure, we messaged Butch and Millie on our group chat. Within thirty minutes they both replied saying that we would get our share soon.

Anyway, the pizza was delicious. I had a limited edition topping, made up of BBQ chicken, a mix of scintillating South American Spices, and splashes of Worcester Sauce. When I arrived back at my house, I came home to a satisfying surprise.

There was a parcel on my bed that was addressed to me! I opened it up, and inside there were two gold bars. There was also a note from Millie. It was a nice feeling when I finally had a share of the treasure. The week that had gone by had been incredibly hectic to say the least. But one thing is for sure: whatever adventure comes my way next, I'll be ready for it.

Printed in Great Britain
by Amazon

18758589R00092